CLOAK AND SPIDER

A Shadowdance Novella

David Dalglish

Table of Contents

Cloak and Spider

Stealing Spoons

Thren Felhorn watched the merchant's stall, his stomach rumbling as he imagined the food he might eat if the score went off as intended. His friend Grayson was already there, asking question after question of the merchant busy trying to sell his wares to a wealthy couple dressed in red silks and fox fur. At best Grayson earned himself a swat at his head, but Thren's dark-skinned friend always ducked aside just before it connected. After one aggravated swipe, and a yell to get lost, Grayson turned toward him and winked before sidling back up to the stall.

That was the signal. Thren kept his head down, his hands in his pockets. Most importantly, he kept his eyes to the ground. Without eye contact, he would be invisible to the populace of the grand city of Mordeina, just one of a hundred orphan boys forced to beg, borrow, and steal for their daily bread. But today Thren planned on eating far better than stale, cracked bread that had gone unsold the day before.

"...the finest silver," he heard the merchant say to the couple as he made exaggerated gestures as if to express his amazement at the quality of his own wares. Thren slid closer, using the couple as a screen for his movements. Head down, eyes low, using just the corners of his vision to guide his movements. When he was almost there, the merchant let out a cry, turning toward where Grayson had tried, and failed, to snag a knife from on display. The merchant, a bearded man with a large belly, let out a roar and swung a meaty fist. This time Grayson did not dodge in time, the fist connecting squarely with his face. Blood splattered down his chest, and he let out a cry as he stumbled to the ground.

"I didn't do nothing!" Grayson cried.

With all eyes on Grayson for that split second, Thren brushed against the lady of the couple, his movements pulling out her dress the tiniest bit, giving him the screen he needed. Arms crossed over his chest, he walked on, not once looking at the merchant busy yelling for a guard. Slid into the folds of his ratty shirt, the metal cool on his skin, were a pair of silver spoons. It took all his control to continue normally, to not smile or show the slightest sign of life. Orphans weren't supposed to know happiness. Happiness was suspicious.

When he reached one of the many exits of the long market street winding through the western half of the city, he dared let out a laugh. He'd made it. Grayson would easily elude whatever guards might come running, and then...

A hand latched on to his shoulder, spinning him about. Thren let out a cry, and he lashed out with his right hand, still holding the spoons. He expected a fat merchant, maybe a guard, but instead a blackened hand caught his own. The skin looked as if it'd been charred in a fire, and the many glittering rings on its fingers made it seem all the more ugly. Thren felt his heart freeze in his chest, felt his breath catch in his throat. The man's hair was a dark umber, his long coat wrapping about his slender frame. After his hand, it was his ears that were most telling, the long ears of an elf with the tops brutally scarred to remove the slender upturned points. Held still by a grip impossibly strong, Thren stared up into the icy blue eyes of a man he knew only by legend.

"It's dangerous to take what isn't yours," Muzien the Darkhand said, "especially when you take from one of *my* merchants."

The grip on Thren's hand tightened, and he released the spoons. The polished silver clattered on the ground, but Muzien did not look at them, nor move to pick them up. Instead he continued to stare, his hand brushing aside a few strands of umber hair that had fallen across his face. Thren kept his mouth shut, knowing nothing he could say would help him now. He was at the man's mercy. Thren gambled that strength was what he needed to show now, not cowardice. Even with that strength, he struggled to meet Muzien's gaze.

"You had help," Muzien said. "Who was it? Tell me his name."

Thren swallowed. Turning on Grayson would gain him nothing, he knew that from the coldness in Muzien's eyes. So he lifted his head, clenched his jaw, and waited.

The reaction came more swiftly than he'd anticipated. Muzien flung him against one of the city's winding walls, the uneven red brick stabbing into his back. Despite his attempt to brace himself, Thren let out a cry. Muzien towered above him, and his hand drifted down to the hilt of a sword strapped to his side.

"How old are you?" he asked.

"Nine," Thren said, remaining on his rear.

"Good, so you can tell the truth if necessary. So let me try this one more time." He slid his sword out of its sheath, just enough to let it catch the light from the midday sun. "Who helped you in your attempt?"

"I was alone," Thren said, figuring that if he was to die he'd at least try to spare his friend. "Did it all on my own."

Muzien stared at him, a long hard gaze that made Thren feel as if he were being dissected.

"Only nine," he said, shaking his head. "And to think I had thought myself beyond surprises. *Alric!* Bring him over."

From around the corner came another man with a similar coat to Muzien's, only he was more heavyset, the muscularity of his frame more obvious. In his arms he lugged Grayson, who was still trying to squirm away.

"Cut it out already," Alric said, dumping Grayson beside Thren. A quick glance showed Grayson's nose was still bleeding a bit, but that was the only real injury he'd suffered from the merchant's hit.

"They were waiting for us, I swear it," Grayson said, springing to his feet. Thren rose as well. He wouldn't die sitting down. Muzien let go of his blade and crossed his arms.

"I have need of servants," he said. "Are you both orphans without family?"

The two glanced at each other.

"We are," Thren said, purposefully leaving out any mention of Grayson's sister. The last thing he wanted to do was drag her into their mess.

"Then you shall live with me, and serve the Sun Guild directly. Is that understood?"

"What if we refuse?" Grayson asked.

Muzien knelt down so they might see eye to eye.

"What makes you think you may refuse?" he asked.

Thren had seen Grayson stand up to the toughest of bullies and the meanest of guards, yet still his friend shrunk beneath that gaze. Grayson lowered his head and nodded to show he understood.

"Good," Muzien said, spinning on his heels. "Alric, take them in and get them cleaned up. The ceremony's almost here, and we have no time to waste."

*

Thren and Grayson had served under Muzien for three days when he led them into the grand dining hall of his Sun Guild's vast headquarters. There were over forty people seated along three rows of tables, with a vast variety of foods atop silver platters before them. Twenty more of the long rectangular tables were empty. Most of the men and women held cups, and Thren saw an opened keg in one corner. Along one side of the room were five thick stained-glass windows, each pane depicting the sun as it marched from dawn to dusk.. Multiple chandeliers hung overhead, dozens of candles in them burning bright. The size of it all left Thren with an uneasy feeling, as if he were overexposed. The dining hall could easily hold two hundred people, if not three, yet right then it felt so empty.

"There," Muzien said, pointing to an empty corner. "I do not need you now, so go wait there until I come for you."

The two boys nodded, having quickly learned that speaking was necessary only if they might misunderstand the order given to them. Thren led the way, and at the corner he slumped down and tried to relax. Overall his time with the Sun Guild had been one of fine food and far nicer clothing, yet he still felt exhausted from the variety of chores, all menial and tedious, that Muzien subjected them to. They were yet to eat their midday meal, too, and seeing the vast banquet spread out before the others left Thren in a foul mood.

"I bet we'll be the ones stuck cleaning all this up," Grayson said, unafraid of being heard due to the great din of celebration from the forty in attendance.

"I bet you're right," Thren muttered back.

At Muzien's entrance many had stood and raised glasses in salute to their guildmaster. Muzien smiled back, showing a kindness neither of the orphans had seen directed their way. The elf took an offered glass, then walked to the center of the table. He lifted his glass and slowly turned so he might look upon all forty.

"Today is the start of a grand beginning," he said. "With your aid I have built a kingdom. Merchants tithe to us for safety. The underworld fears to cross us, for our wrath is as sure as the rising sun. The priests turn blind eyes to our deeds, the king pretends we are but stories told by foolish men. Nine decades I have ruled, and for decades more I plan to rule from the throne I have fashioned out of silver and gold. Yet the world is fickle, and the paths we walk ever dangerous. Every king, no matter how great his reign, must have an heir. For that I have summoned you, so think well on the privilege such an invitation demands. Think well on the seriousness of the position, the cost of such a gift."

He turned to where Alric stood by the door, and Alric pulled it open with a creak.

"The door is open," Muzien said, and he drank. "The door will always be open."

And with that he set down his glass, bowed to them all, and walked out of the room.

Awkward silence followed as the forty men and women looked to one another, unsure of what to do and what was expected of them.

"Should we go?" Grayson whispered to Thren as the confused chatter grew louder.

"He said he'd summon us," Thren said, as if it were obvious. "So until then, we stay."

And so they stayed.

———

*

Three hours later the first of them left.

Thren had spent the time wandering among the tables. The people assumed he was there to serve them, and he did nothing to disabuse them of that assumption. He fetched drinks from the keg, mostly, shifted plates of food from one table to another if asked, and stole bites whenever no one was watching. All the while he listened to the men and women talk, attaching names to the various faces. He was filling yet another mug from the keg when he heard the squeal of a chair scraping across the wood floor, followed by a bit of good-natured ribbing.

"You all know I'd be shit for a leader," said the man, an overweight fellow Thren hadn't caught the name of. "You can all stick around, settle this among yourselves. As for me, I need to piss more than I ever have in my life."

His words were spoken in jest, but as he exited the open door a pall came over those remaining. Thren felt it was as real as the cup in his hand. He brought it back to its owner, a pretty woman with dark hair and brown eyes by the name of Jezelle.

"Why didn't you fill it?" she asked as he set it down before her.

"Can't," Thren said.

"Can't?"

He shrugged. "The keg is empty."

"You hear that?" said a man beside Jezelle. "The keg's empty! What in the fiery Abyss are we to drink now?"

"Give me a few minutes," another shouted back at him. "I'll give you a cup of warm yellow ale you'll love."

Still more joking, but Thren heard the worry in their voices. There was nothing left to drink but what remained in the people's cups, and nowhere to relieve oneself unless one left the room. The day dragged on into evening, and several more stood up.

"Fuck it," said a man, Jared.

"I'm coming with you," said a woman at his side.

The two strode for the door, and they were quickly joined by five others. Those who remained quickly checked the cups of those who had left, the first hint of the hoarding to come.

"We should do something," Thren said as he took a seat by Grayson in the corner, watching as several more made their way to the door.

"Not yet," Grayson said, his eyes on the tables. "For now we wait."

"Wait for what?"

"The groups to form."

Two hours later the number had stabilized at twenty-five. There were no jokes now beyond a few forced laughs. Thren saw Grayson had been right about the groups. There were three major ones, all fairly equally divided, and they positioned themselves into a loose triangle amid the huge dining hall tables. Thren stayed in the corner with Grayson, watching, going out only once to retrieve a beige bowl made of plaster. Slowly he tapped it on the ground, methodically weakening one side.

He was so busy chipping away, watching the cracks spread, he almost didn't catch the fight.

"I think we've all had enough of this farce," said Crion, a middle-aged man with a long sword strapped to his belt. He commanded the largest of the three groups, and he had a dozen gold earrings in his left ear, signifying kills he'd made in the name of the Sun Guild.

"You're welcome to leave," said Jezelle, who sat next to the obvious leader of the second group, a muscular man with a shaved head named Terk .

Crion grinned at Jezelle, revealing a mouth full of black teeth.

"I won't be the one leaving. You all will. We know what's going on. The cowards have left, which leaves just us, and if hunger and thirst don't drive us out, then that means it'll be a blade."

"Muzien will come back for us before then," said Ulgrad, an older man with gray hair and a row of daggers around his waist. Thren had found it difficult to identify the clear leader of the third group, but Grayson insisted Ulgrad was the one.

"Are you so certain?" Crion asked. "Tell me, which of the stories of the Darkhand you grew up listening to told of his *mercy*, or his *compassion*?

"Yet those who kill fellow members of the guild hang at dawn," Ulgrad argued. "We'll solve this somehow, but it won't be through something as stupid and inelegant as a slaughter."

"You're just a damn bully," Jezelle shouted. "You won't scare us out."

Crion turned his ugly grin toward Jezelle.

"Say that again when you're not draped over the arm of your muscle-bound fuck toy, Jezelle. I beg of you."

Terk rose to his feet, and he drew a long blade off his back and held it before him.

"Insult her again," Terk said, his deep voice rumbling. "I beg of *you*."

"Enough!" Ulgrad shouted. "Put the blades away. For all we know Muzien is watching us this very moment. Who here wants to confront the Darkhand later as the one who caused the deaths of fellow Sun guildmembers? Who here thinks they'll walk away alive with that blood on their hands?"

———

The tension was tight, and all three groups readied their weapons. They needed a spark, just a spark. Thren felt his heart skip a beat as he stood, slowly getting closer to the three long rows of tables, and the groups seated therein. It was a gamble, and if it failed he'd look like a fool—or worse, earn their wrath. But if he was right...

"He's got a bow!" he shouted, pointing at Ulgrad's group. "He's gonna shoot!"

And before they could think on it, before their conscious minds could take over, Grayson hurled a spoon from behind Ulgrad's group. It sailed over their heads, and that sign of movement, that flash of something hurtling through the air, spurred them into action. Crion led the way, tearing into Ulgrad's group with the wild fury of a barbarian.

Terk let out a cry, and at first Thren thought he'd go barging in as well, but it seemed the man had a mind to go along with his muscles. His sword swung out wide, holding back the rest of his group. Instead he issued orders, sending three of his men off running, then guided the rest to the far wall. Thren brought his attention back to the fight, watching as Crion's sword cut and slashed with impressive skill. They might have been even in numbers, but Ulgrad had attracted those without a desire to fight, and against the brutal rush they crumbled and died. Two threw down their weapons, and only those two survived.

"Out the door," Crion screamed at them, blood splashed across his shirt. "Out, now!"

The two hurried to leave.

"And take this with you!"

Crion hurled Ulgrad's head after them. It rolled along the ground, coming to a stop underneath one of the tables. The two men glared at it but said nothing, only exited the room. Thren and Grayson huddled in the corner, counting. Seventeen left now, not counting themselves.

Jezelle kissed her protector's face, then winked at Crion.

"Hope you didn't wear yourself out," she said. The two groups were on opposite sides of the dining hall now, and it looked as if neither was ready to cross just yet.

"Still plenty of time," Crion said.

"Indeed," Terk said, and he gestured to the table directly before him. "But I do not think time is on your side."

During the battle the runners from his group had rushed out, grabbing food from the tables away from the fight. Their pile was thrice the size of Crion's. When Crion realized this, Terk let out a grin.

"Just try," he said as several of his men tipped over nearby tables, forming a barricade beside the wall. The tables were long and flat, and they fitted together nicely to form a waist-high wall. Others began rifling bodies, taking weapons.

Crion's chest rose and fell as he glanced over the growing fortification.

"Come on," he said, glaring, leading the rest of his own group to begin a similar barricade.

Thren and Grayson whispered in the corner as outside the sun finished setting, leaving them with only the light of the candles, candles rapidly nearing the end of their life.

"What now?" asked Grayson.

"I'm not sure," said Thren. "I was hoping all three would fight. Terk's proving...formidable."

"Should we try to join one of the groups?"

Thren shrugged. "Neither would have us."

"Then what do we do?"

At that, Thren looked to his cracked bowl, then to the fortifications of tables. Behind them he could hear both sides preparing shifts for sleep.

"We could always leave," he said.

Grayson looked to the open door, shook his head.

"My gut says leaving's a bad idea. Muzien wants us to stay, so we stay."

Thren tapped his bowl.

"Well then," he said, "let's tip the scales."

*

It was well past midnight when the last of the candles sputtered, flickered for a moment, and then died. The only light remaining came from the stained-glass windows, the moonlight weak and dark as it filtered through them. In the shadows Thren crawled, bowl in hand. Before him were three overturned tables, creating a haphazard wall. Only a single man stayed on watch, and what little Thren could see of his face showed him to be very nervous.

Thren crawled along the wall opposite the windows, and as he pressed his body against one of the tables, he knew he would be all but invisible to the guard. Invisible would not be enough, though. Crawling over the overturned table and into their sleeping ground would risk too much movement, and worse, too much sound. The man standing before the middle overturned table had a dagger drawn, and he was turning from side to side, searching for the slightest sign of an attack from the opposing group.

And that's when Grayson kicked hard against a table on the far side of the room.

"Shit," Thren heard the guard mutter, spinning in that direction. Thren counted to two, then vaulted himself over the defense. Right on time, another loud wooden thud sounded as Grayson flung his weight against a table. Thren landed, and he froze when he did. He could barely see the faces of those sleeping along the ground, not enough to pick out their leader, but he didn't need to. All he needed was the vague shapes, the outlines of where he could and could not step. Making sure his breaths were slow and even, he worked his way to the very center of the miniature fortification. The man on watch had his back to him, and in the ensuing silence kept his gaze outward, tense, waiting for just one more signal that the other group was advancing so he might wake his own.

In the very center Thren found him, just as he'd thought he would. Slowly he took the bowl, careful to hold it by the proper end. One side was still smooth, but the other…

The other he jammed upward into the soft flesh of Terk's throat, the sharp broken ridges digging in deep. Blood poured into the bowl as Terk startled awake, his arms flailing, his legs kicking. Thren released the bowl and ran, nearly vaulting with each step. He didn't care if he stepped on others this time, nor if they woke. All that mattered was keeping his movements long and fast so that no one might grab a hold of his leg or arm.

He heard cries, warning, accusations of betrayal and ambush as he made his way to the corner farthest from the windows.

"Did you get him?" Grayson asked, and his voice was like a ghost in the darkness.

"I think he'll die," Thren answered. "We'll know come morning…"

*

Thren didn't remember falling asleep, but he must have, for Grayson was shaking him awake.

"Get up," he heard his friend saying. "It'll start soon."

He did so with his heart racing, and he berated himself for being so stupid. At least it seemed Grayson had watched over him, ensuring no one sneaked up on them while he slept in the darkness. As he squinted he saw the sun had just begun to rise, casting light into the room so all might see. Crion was eating with the rest of his band, finishing off the bulk of their food. They seemed in a jovial mood.

"Aren't you going to have a bite, Terk?" Crion shouted out to the other group, which was huddled far closer together as it ate.

"Fuck off," Jezelle shouted back.

This seemed to give Crion pause, and he put down the apple he held. His hand fell to his sword as he stepped through a small gap in their overturned table wall.

"Terk?" he asked. "Where are you, Terk?"

When the other man did not answer, Crion looked back to his own band.

"Draw your weapons," he told them, and they did. Jezelle saw this from the other side, swore, and drew her own.

"We can still hold you off," she said as those with her prepared for combat. Yet it sounded as if even she did not believe it, and Crion certainly didn't.

"No, you can't," he said. "So who of you killed him? Did you think to take him out now, before he ended up winning? I'd say you got ahead of yourselves."

"I said get back!" Jezelle screamed.

"No!" Crion roared. "You're beaten now, and you know it. Terk's the only reason I wasn't eating my breakfast out of your skulls as a bowl, and now the fucker's dead."

Thren and Grayson kept their backs to the wall, watching as Crion's band slowly descended on Jezelle's.

They already a numbers advantage, and without Terk, it was obvious no one could stand against Crion in a fight.

"I'm not sure this will work," Grayson said, anticipating another battle.

"Just wait," Thren said, hoping he was right.

When Jezelle's group was fully surrounded, Crion smiled and pointed to the door.

"I'll let all of you walk out of here right now," he told them. "Just throw down your weapons, and there'll be no hard feelings."

They looked to one another, and it was obvious to Thren that they were going to accept.

"Not worth it," said one, and he tossed a dagger beyond their wall. Several others immediately followed, and the sound of metal clanged throughout the dining hall.

"Not yet," Crion said, stepping in the way of the first who tried to flee. "She stays. The others of you can go."

Jezelle's face paled, but the others with her had no argument. They left her standing alone behind the tables, still holding her dagger. Once the seven men exited the open doorway, Crion approached with his sword drawn.

"Drop the dagger and I'll make it quick," he told her.

"You could just let me go," she said.

"I could," Crion said. "But I won't. When I take over, you'll only be a thorn in my side. Now drop it, or I'll make sure your death lasts a very, very long time."

After a moment of meeting Crion's stare, she lifted her arm and let the dagger drop. Crion smiled.

"Good girl," he said.

His sword lunged out, piercing the base of her throat, and then pulled back. She stood there, glaring even as she died, her legs giving out. Her forehead hit the table with a sickening crunch, leaving a splatter of reddish gore along its top edge.

Crion wiped his sword, sheathed it, and then turned to the rest, a giant grin on his face.

"We did it!" he said. "All of you will be well rewarded for years to come, I promise."

Beside Thren, Grayson slumped against the wall.

"Crion won," he said. "We need to either hide or run, because he'll kill us next."

"Not yet," Thren whispered.

The eight other men didn't seem to be sharing in Crion's rejoicing. The smile on the middle-aged man's face slowly faded away.

"Step out," he said to them. "All of you. It's over."

"Who said it's over?" one of them asked.

"I ain't leaving," said another.

Thren felt his heart begin to race as Crion slowly realized what was happening. The others backed away, none willing to attack him, but it was clear they were no longer on his side. With a sudden burst of movement, all nine made for the two remaining piles of food. Crion stabbed one of them through the back, yet when he managed to reach his table barely any food was left. He hovered over it, guarding it as three others split for various sections of wall. The same happened at the other table, men scooping up stale bread and browning fruit and seeking out a place of safety. Two more died in that skirmish, a small man with beady eyes and dark hair thrusting a dagger into the necks of the slowest two, a man and a woman who had scooped up more food than they should have, their full arms slowing their defense until it was too late.

"Six left," Thren whispered when the chaos subsided. "It's a whole new game."

After so many leaving or dying that morning, it seemed the remaining six were content to stay in their respective sections of the room, each with a table or two to give protection. Thren and Grayson did their best to lie low, but with such smaller numbers, it was getting harder to go unnoticed.

"Hey," said one of the men, the beady-eyed one named Nolan. He sat cross-legged in the center of the room, as if unafraid of the others. He looked tired, as did all the rest. Once the rush of the earlier conflict had faded, and the morning stretched into day, they'd all sagged in their seats or against the wall.

Thren looked away, pretended not to notice Nolan was talking to him.

"Hey, you two little shits," Nolan called.

Thren elbowed Grayson in the side, waking him up. The two had slept in shifts, alternating each hour, at least their best estimates of an hour. Grayson woke, immediately noticed Nolan glaring at them. Neither gave the dark-haired man an answer.

"Those two are still here?" Crion asked from his corner. He laughed as if it were the funniest thing. "Got balls, I'll give you that, but I think it's time you two got out before something bad happens."

Neither moved. Nolan muttered a curse, got to his feet. He brandished a long dirk in his small pale fingers.

"You know," he said, "I could use a bit of fun."

Despite how alert he seemed, Thren knew his friend was still waking up, and he needed the attention on him instead. Besides, he was smaller, and faster.

"Go ask Crion for some fun," Thren said. "I heard he likes your type. Skinny and dumb."

When Nolan rushed him, he dove to the side, rolling underneath the legs of a table and bolting toward the middle of the room. The man chased as the others laughed and watched. Thren weaved his way about, scampering along the floor when he needed to, running along the tops of tables if necessary to get away. It didn't matter to him how pathetic he looked, he just had to survive.

"Can't kill a little child?" Thren heard someone yell, and Thren purposefully veered along the wall in the yeller's direction. He scooped up a piece of shit from a spot several had used to relieve themselves and then spun, flinging the brown sludge behind him. He hit Nolan square in the chest, earning himself a colorful tirade of curses.

"Just fucking...stand...*still!*"

Nolan hurled his dirk. Thren dropped to his stomach, heard it thud into a table above him. Scrambling, leaving brown smeared handprints on the floor beneath him, he made his way back to Grayson, who had never moved from his spot. Nolan, as if realizing how vulnerable he was with his weapon thrown, quickly retrieved it, then made his way back toward his food. The eyes of the others were on him, and Thren knew how bad, how weak, it must have looked to fail to kill a nine-year-old boy.

Too bad, thought Thren.

"He almost got you twice," Grayson said as Thren slumped against the wall beside him.

"Almost don't count," Thren said.

Grayson laughed, elbowed him in the side.

"Your turn. I got this."

More than relieved, and with his head pounding from hunger, thirst, and exhaustion, Thren closed his eyes and did his best to sleep.

Except he couldn't. He felt Grayson tense up beside him, and he reopened his eyes to see Crion was on the hunt. The man was calmly walking about the dining hall, judging everyone's reactions. Several backed away, sliding in the opposite direction. Only Nolan remained where he was, twirling his dirk in his left hand.

"Don't test me," Nolan said to Crion. "I'm in a pissed-off mood as it is."

"You could always leave," Crion said, walking around him as if Nolan were a mad dog on a leash. "As our brilliant leader said, the door is always open."

Crion veered to the side, purposefully putting his back to Nolan as if daring him to throw his dirk. For a moment Thren thought he would, but then Nolan backed down. Instead Crion approached another man, this one heavyset and bearded. Thren struggled to remember his name, but then Crion spoke it aloud.

"You've always been a good friend, Jarvis," Crion said to the bearded man. "So why do you stay so far away from me?"

Jarvis scratched at his rust-colored beard. In his other hand he held up a thick short sword.

"Been a good friend to you because it paid to be your good friend," Jarvis said, his voice carrying a thick Kerran accent. "But not now, not anymore. We all started out equal in here, and one of us is walking out a king. And you know what, Crion? I sure as shit don't want to see it be you that comes out on top."

"You won't see it," Crion told him. "Because you'll be dead first."

Jarvis had been ready for the attack, Thren had no doubt about that. But being ready for it and being able to survive it were two very different things, as Jarvis found out. Crion took a step closer, then jammed his arm forward as if to thrust. Jarvis flung his short sword around to parry, but Crion was too fast. He sidestepped, pulling his sword back and out of the way of the parry. Jarvis's sword continued without any steel for it to hit, and as it smacked against the rough wood floor it let out a loud thunk, the sound broken only by the scream Jarvis made when Crion's sword thrust deep into his chest.

Crion twisted once, pulled the blade free, then glanced to the others.

"Fucking cowards," he said, seeing not a one had dared make a move on him. "It's only a matter of time."

He sheathed his sword, stalked back toward his corner.

"Only five," Thren whispered as he closed his eyes, leaning his weight against Grayson. "Now just five…"

When he woke an hour later to Grayson jabbing him in the side, he wished he could sleep longer. His stomach hurt, his headhurt worse, and he'd have begged on his hands and knees for a drink of water for his dry, sticky tongue. But he thought it best to put that aside when he heard his friend speak.

"Now four," he said. "Nolan killed Uriah while he slept."

"Why'd he sleep?" Thren asked, rubbing at his eyes.

"Don't think he did all night," Grayson said, shrugging. His brown eyes were locked on the far left wall, where Uriah's body lay slumped, throat cut, blood lazily dripping down his neck and onto his pale-yellow shirt. The little food the man had stored up was now in Nolan's pile, which was shrinking rapidly as he wolfed down what he had.

"Going to give yourself a stomachache," said one of the remaining four, a thin man with a badly scarred face. Thren recognized him from before being recruited by Muzien: he was a soft-spoken man named Logan. Logan was one of a dozen fences throughout Mordeina, and whenever Thren stole something particularly expensive, and therefore hard to sell, it was to Logan he went. Didn't matter if its previous owner's blood was still wet upon the merchandise, Logan would buy it. He always seemed happy enough, but Thren had learned quickly from the other boys to stay away and reject any offers of a meal. Logan's tastes ran young, and according to the whispers, it was rare for one of his boys to return to the streets afterward.

"Better from food than a sword in the gut," Nolan said. "Isn't that right, Uriah? Uriah! Oh, right, dead. I forgot."

"Just shut up," Crion said. "You aren't as funny as you think."

"And you're not as good as you think," Nolan said, lifting a cracked muffin into the air as a toast. "To your amazing skills, Crion, and to your soon ignoble death. May you as a corpse be more entertaining than you were in life."

"You all laugh," said the fourth man. He had long red hair, a scar that ran across the bridge of his nose, and hardly any teeth. His name was Phillip. "But you've missed the real joke. It ain't us four that is going to win."

"Then who will?" Crion asked, rubbing at his face, which had long dark circles beneath the eyes.

"Yes, please tell us," Nolan said. "I hate not being in on a joke."

In answer, Phillip pointed right at Thren and Grayson. Thren felt his insides tighten. The last thing he wanted was attention.

"Those two," Phillip said. "They been hiding out the whole time, sleeping when we can't, grabbing food we've left behind. They'll outlast all of us, I'm sure of it."

"You're out of your mind," Logan said. "Two kids outlast the four of us? The lack of drink is getting to you, my friend."

Phillip laughed at the word *friend*.

"Perhaps," he said. "But here we are, six of us if we include them, and how many before them are gone? Twenty? Thirty?"

All four were looking at the boys now. Thren slowly rose to his feet, feeling his throat constrict. Grayson stood likewise, and Thren could tell by the look on his face that his plan was simple: whichever way Thren fled, Grayson would flee the other.

"This is stupid," Crion said, grabbing his sword and slipping around his wall of tables. "Nolan, they embarrassed you once, so do us both a favor and kill whoever slips around either side of me. It may sting going into the Abyss knowing one of you three will inherit the Sun Guild, but I sure as shit won't let it be these two little snots."

Thren took a breath, and he looked to either side. They were against the windows along the long wall, with Nolan directly across from them in the middle, and Logan to their right. Crion approached from their left, tapping his sword against his pant leg as he walked. The other two stepped closer, readying their own weapons. It seemed whatever good humor they'd just shown was gone, a tired resolve coming over them. Thren's eyes kept bouncing among the three, trying to figure out whom he could slip by most easily.

"We're only here because Muzien ordered us to stay," Thren said, hoping maybe to stall them. "That's all."

"You want to live, you go run out that door," Crion said, still advancing. "Otherwise stand still and die like a man. It'll hurt less that way."

"Run past him at the same time," Grayson whispered. "He can't get us both."

It was the only plan Thren could think of with his exhausted mind. Convinced he was about to die, he sucked in a breath, watching for the moment when Crion moved to strike so he could dive out of the way and then flee.

He never had the chance. Nolan let out a gasp, jerked forward.

"Ah fuck," he said as blood ran down his chest, a point of steel poking out between his ribs. He collapsed, revealing Phillip standing behind him with the bloodied blade. He stared at Crion, his face an emotionless mask. Crion froze at the display, then took a step back as both Logan and Phillip approached.

"I'm not one to share power," Phillip said. "But for Logan, I think I'd be willing to try. A fortune split in half is still a fortune. Three ways, though?"

"Three ways is no good," Logan said, holding high his own dirk. Thren watched them pass by before him, forgotten once more. He and Grayson had merely been a distraction to use against Crion and Nolan, he knew, and he was too tired to decide if he was flattered or annoyed that they'd ever been considered a threat, however momentarily.

Crion continued backing up, stopping only after he'd slipped through the gap between two of the tables of his meager fortification. Phillip and Logan stood side by side as they neared, weapons at the ready. Thren looked over, caught Grayson staring, and knew they had to act fast.

"Come on," he said, elbowing his friend and pointing. "We don't have much time!"

As Thren moved, he kept the three in the corner of his eye, cheering on Crion. If he could at least kill one of the other two, then there might still be a chance…

The fight began without a word spoken among them. Phillip took a step forward, putting him just within arm's reach, and stabbed. He did it without breaking stride, with Logan still at his side. As Crion brought his sword up to block, Logan leaped over the table, attempting to clear its top. He misjudged the height, banging his shins on the side. As he toppled forward Crion hit once, twice against Phillip's blade, forcing an opening, and then dove to the ground. He landed with his elbow slamming against Logan's throat, all his weight driving down on it. After that he rolled, avoiding a desperate lunge by Phillip over the wall.

And then he was back on his feet, a wolfish grin on his dirty face. There was victory in his eyes, and no doubt Phillip saw it. The table still between them, they engaged once more, swords flashing, but Crion was the better. When his sword pierced Phillip's throat, and the blade fell from the dying man's hand, it sounded as if he almost tried to sigh.

After that, Crion walked back over to where Logan lay, still futilely gasping for air, and drove his sword into his side.

"About fucking time," Crion said.

When he turned their way, Thren and Grayson had armed themselves from Nolan's now abandoned stash. They held their slender knives before them, up and ready for the attack. Crion saw them and laughed.

"You two?" he asked, gesturing around the dining hall. There were bodies everywhere, the smell of them rank and coupled with the smell of piss and shit from so many forced to make do without anywhere to defecate. Tables were overturned, food lay smashed into the hard floor, and seeming to cover everything was the blood of the dead. The only clean place was before the exit to the room, and its open door. "Do you really think I'm scared of you two, after all this?"

"We're not scared of *you*," Grayson said. Thren's heart pounded, but for the first time since everything had started, he felt in control of matters.

"And you don't have to be afraid of us," Thren said. "You just need to die."

Crion approached them, weaving his way around the tables. Grayson and Thren shared a look, then stepped apart. When Crion closed in on Thren, Grayson drifted around to the side, putting himself behind the older man and out of his line of sight. Crion sensed the tactic, and he looked none too pleased.

"Think you're going to surround me?" he asked. "I've killed dozens of men far faster and better than you."

Thren didn't waste his breath arguing. When Crion moved to attack him, instead of attempting to fight him, he only turned and fled as fast as his legs could carry him. He dove into a roll, kicking out of it to curl around one of the tables, and then ran to the far side of the room. Crion tried to chase, but he was bigger, older, and the obstacles were far more of an annoyance to him. Thren put his back to the wall, sweat running down his neck and his stomach sick, but he'd gained space on his attacker.

"Slippery devils, aren't you?" Crion asked. He turned, saw Grayson shadowing him. "But you can't run away from me forever."

We'll see about that, thought Thren.

This time Crion went after Grayson, whirling on his feet in an attempt to surprise him. But Grayson had spent the past few years surviving based on his ability to flee from angry merchants, and he knew how to move, how to roll underneath a bench, how to keep his head low and his feet moving regardless of how slick the ground was from spilled blood and food. Crion lost him, and he stood alone in the center of the dining hall, with Thren and Grayson each on the far side.

"Muzien!" Crion shouted, spinning in place. "I know you can see us! End this madness already! You know who your winner is."

No answer.

Swearing, Crion turned back to Thren, paused. A grin spread across his face, revealing his ugly black teeth, and he went to one of the many weapon caches scattered about the room and picked up several knives.

"Come on then," he said, readying one. "You might run fast, but how well can you dodge?"

Thren tensed as the gray-haired man took careful steps closer, one hand holding his sword, the other readying a knife to throw. Thren watched, watched, and then dove to his knees one way, only to immediately roll the other. The knife thudded against the wall beside him, the wooden handle cracking and breaking. Then he was running, and he heard Crion's footsteps behind him, heard his heavy breathing. Relying on his instincts, he dove to the side at the first table, rolling underneath as yet another knife clacked against the ground.

To Grayson he ran, nearly throwing himself against the wall beside his friend. Spinning around, he dared let out a laugh.

"This isn't a game!" Crion screamed, grabbing one of the knives.

"If it is," Thren said, struggling to catch his breath, "I think we're winning."

Crion hurled the dagger at Grayson, who dodged left into Thren's side. Luck was with him, for the throw had anticipated his movement, except to the right. Both sprinted away, Thren trailing behind Grayson. Crion swung his sword, missed, and Thren saw his opening. Instead of fleeing he dove straight at Crion, jamming upward with his slender dagger. The tip cut into Crion's side, tearing flesh. Thren released the weapon so he could run, ducking underneath a frantic blow.

A smile on his face, Thren reached the other side of the dining hall. Grayson saw the smile, knew what it meant.

"You got him?" he asked.

Thren turned, nodded.

"I did," he said.

Crion held his side, trying to stem the blood. The cut wasn't too deep, but Thren knew there'd be no way for the man to bandage it. They wouldn't give him the time. Crion released his hand, held it up bloody before them, and let out a primal cry. He charged them, but this time there were no games, no letting him get close so they might look for an opening. They stayed on the opposite side no matter where he went. Crion stumbled, he bumped into tables, he slipped once on a pool of spilled wine left by some nameless member of the Sun Guild. All the while his weakened body lost blood.

Thren felt ready to pass out himself, but he carried on. Just a little while longer, he told himself. Just a tiny bit more.

At last Crion slumped to the ground in the middle of the dining hall, sword limp in his right hand. Thren and Grayson stalked over to him, as if they were lions and he a wounded animal. Crion saw them coming, and he chuckled.

"Fuck you, Phillip," he breathed.

When the boys were close he flung his sword at Grayson, but the throw was errant, the weapon not designed for such use. It clattered along the ground, leaving him helpless.

———

Thren leaped at him first, then pulled away when Crion tried to punch him in the face. Grayson jumped him from behind then, stabbing the man's back repeatedly. As he screamed and tried to reach around to grab Grayson, Thren took the opening and dove in, stabbing the man's throat as Crion screamed his denial. When he pulled the dagger free, blood poured across his hands from the gaping wound. Grayson jumped away, and together, each soaked in blood, they watched the man die.

"Last one," Grayson said, and he looked ready to vomit.

"Not quite," Thren said, and he met his friend's eye. They each held a weapon, each stained with another man's blood. Thren opened his mouth to say something, but didn't know what to say. Grayson, however, was the better of them.

"No," he said. "It is."

He dropped his dagger.

Thren took a step closer, grip tightening on his own dagger. This was his chance, a way to ensure that Muzien would not be disappointed in him. But after all they'd done, all they had endured in both the streets of Mordeina and the dining hall of the Sun Guild...

Thren dropped his dagger.

"Enough!"

Together they turned around and fell to their knees as Muzien the Darkhand stepped into the room. His face was a calm mask, but his eyes seemed to shine.

"You were but a gamble and a dream," he said as he approached. "Never did I believe you would succeed. But you did, you two did. The Sun Guild's future has never been brighter than at this very moment."

Thren felt something burning in his chest, and he wondered what it was. Pain? Hunger?

It felt good, though. It felt like worth. It felt like pride. It felt as if a legend had just given him meaning and purpose. When he glanced at Grayson, he saw that same understanding revealing itself as a giant grin on his dark-skinned friend's face.

"Follow me," Muzien said, taking them toward the exit. There seemed to be a bounce to his step, and an excitement to his voice. "You both will need to recover, and I'll ensure you have food and drink ready for you in your rooms."

They stepped out the door, and as they did Thren let out a gasp.

All around the door lay the bodies of dozens of men and women, all those who had left earlier. They had died the exact same way, their throats slit, no doubt denying them their dying screams. Thren looked to Muzien, and he felt growing in his addled brain an understanding of just what type of man their lives were now sworn to, of what kind of kingdom he expected to build.

"Why?" he dared ask.

Muzien frowned at the bodies, as if he hadn't noticed their presence until Thren asked about them.

"The door was a gift for the weak, nothing more. A man or woman unwilling to risk everything is someone I do not want in the ranks of my guild."

He turned, knelt before the two so they might see eye to eye. His presence held Thren captive, the strength of his will a frightening portent of all to come.

"In the coming days, you will discover whatever limits your body had were merely lies," he said. "In the coming months, I will subject you to what other men might call torture. In the coming years, you will learn to how to bring death to the invincible, how to wield a blade with the skill of a god. Every king must have his heirs, and I will have

—

heirs worthy of my legend. You will know pain, you will know fear, and at times you will cry out for death to spare you."

Muzien stood, beckoned them with his blackened hand.

"Never forget," he told them, "that the door is always open. Never forget, my children, that in your time of suffering, you chose not to step through it."

Stealing Hearts

"This feels like a lot of effort for a simple party," Marion Lightborn said as the carriage rolled through the crowded streets of Mordeina. "Will it really be as dazzling as you say?"

Kyle Garland sat opposite her in the carriage, and he gave her a patronizing smile.

"How many times must I tell you, it is not a simple party."

Marion shifted the length of her skirt, made of a fine red silk that came to a stop just above her knee. With her sitting, it had pulled even higher, and she caught Kyle stealing glances, no doubt hoping to see beyond the dark skin of her thighs.

"Let me count," she said, putting a hand to her chin and pretending to think hard. "At least twice a day the past month you've bragged about how great this Kensgold thing will be, at least three times a day told me of its amazing importance. Oh dear me, I fear my little head will not be able to count that high, after all."

Kyle shifted in his seat, never comfortable when he was being mocked no matter how lightly. He ran a hand through his long dark hair, a nervous tic of his.

"My dear, if you just want me to put your nerves at ease, I assure you that the evening will be worthwhile, even for you."

Marion batted her eyes at him.

"What do you mean, even for me?"

"I mean that I go because it is expected," Kyle said. The carriage hit a bump, and the jolt knocked his right elbow against the side. He sucked in air through his gritted teeth, then let it out with a curse. With his left hand he rubbed a ring on his right forefinger, one containing an enormous ruby set into an elaborate band of gold, the rubbing another nervous tic of his.

"Expected," he resumed. "When all the families of the Trifect gather, it's career suicide not to attend if at all possible, this one in particular. It's the first Kensgold held west of Neldar, which means anyone with even the slightest reputation will be begging, borrowing, and stealing to make it inside. I'll have a dozen new trade contracts for our finest leaf and wine shipping east within a week of the Kensgold's end. Perhaps for you it'll be…duller, but at least the food will be good, and each Kensgold has a wide variety of entertainment. Surely a juggler or storyteller…"

"A juggler!" Marion interrupted. "Praise the gods, I might get to see a juggler!"

Kyle laughed, and he pinched her knee.

"Complain all you want, but I assure you, tonight will be fun."

Marion smiled at him.

"I hope so," she said.

The carriage rolled to a stop, and Kyle glanced out the window.

"We're here," he said. "Do your best to behave."

"Behave?" Marion asked. "And to think you always seem to be trying your best to have me *not* behave. Or is that only for the bedroom?"

The man's neck flushed red, and he did not respond as he opened the door. After stepping out, he turned and offered her his hand. She took it, then curled her arm around his and nestled her neck against his shoulder. Her dark hair spilled down along the front of his white sleeve, a startling contrast. When she stole a glance at him, he looked so pleased his head was ready to burst. Marion knew what she was to Kyle, a pretty decoration for him to show off to his friends and colleagues, but it didn't bother her much. Stealing a glance at her own red dress, she had to admit she made a fine decoration, one to be envious of indeed.

"Master," said a voice behind them. "The guards are many, and the area safe, so long as you stay within the walls."

Marion turned to see Kyle's two private bodyguards hopping down from the driver's seat of the carriage after a servant rushed up to take over. Both were female, and wore tightly fitted black shirts, slender pants, and thick boots of dark leather. Strapped to their sides were long curved daggers. Most disconcerting to Marion were the featureless masks covering their faces, smooth and white. Only their eyes were visible, and it was the eyes Marion used to distinguish between them. One had green eyes, the other brown. It was Green who was talking, her voice slightly muffled by her mask.

"I'm glad you approve," Kyle told her. "Though I still want you close. The last thing I need is someone eyeing the Heart of Ker and getting sticky fingers."

"You worry about nothing," Marion said, squeezing his arm and urging him along. "Now come. I want to find myself a juggler."

The three wealthy families of the Trifect all lived in the east, but they still owned many homes and businesses all throughout Dezrel. Before them was a great mansion owned by Maynard Gemcroft, the place alight with torches burning behind colored glass. The grounds between the wall and the mansion were filled with men and women talking, all in their very finest outfits. Servants flitted everywhere, carrying a seemingly endless horde of things to eat and drink. At the gate Kyle bowed to the middle-aged advisor who checked everyone's invitations.

"I don't need to present *my* invitation, do I, Bertram?" Kyle asked when it was their turn.

"Lord Garland," said Bertram. "No, you do not, for I sent yours personally. It is your wine I prefer above all others when a hard day needs to be put behind me."

He beckoned for them to pass through the soldiers guarding the gate, and together the group of four passed. Once they were inside, Marion saw Kyle's eyes begin to wander. At first they went to the older men scattered about, wealthy traders who had built vast empires across the land of Dezrel. After that to the many women wearing silken outfits that more often than not enhanced, and hid little of, their curvaceous bodies. They clung to the arms of their men, mouths closed, eyes alight, as if being in their very presence was a blessed gift. It made Marion sick to think that she was one of them.

"Is this where we part ways?" Marion asked as Kyle led her to a group of five men standing about the lawn, drinking wine from tall glasses.

"Are you sure?" Kyle asked, looking her over. She could tell he wasn't sure she'd been at his side long enough for her to be easily labeled as his, but she did not care.

"Yes," she said, gently slipping from his arm. "Enjoy your talks and deals. I need a bit of wine in my stomach before I will enjoy my time."

She made her way through the crowd, careful not to brush against anyone. The last thing she wanted was for someone to initiate conversation with her. Finding the nearest platter of wine carried by a servant, she snagged a glass and then looked for a table somewhere. There were dozens set about, mostly occupied, but she found one in the corner with only two seats, both empty. Sitting in one with her back to the wall of a garden, she sipped her wine. It was weaker than she'd expected, but at least it tasted phenomenal. Distant music of violins and cellos wafted over her, and she closed her eyes to try to relax.

"Is this seat taken?" a man's voice interrupted her thoughts to ask.

"Perhaps," she said, opening her eyes, "depending on who is seeking to claim it."

Before her was a well-dressed man with short blond hair and intense blue eyes. He was young, seventeen, perhaps eighteen at most. His vest was slightly open, and she could tell through the thin white shirt beneath that he was fit. At his waist was a short sword, its sheath tied shut with a comically oversized white ribbon.

"It's not the chair I'm hoping for," he said, still standing. His voice was deep, commanding. "But the company instead."

"Then have the chair," she said. "We'll decide on the company as we go along."

He slid into the seat, then leaned back. The man openly stared at her, and she realized she'd not been told his name.

"Will you not introduce yourself?" she asked.

"My name is Thren," he said. "Of a family of no importance, I assure you, but at the same time the importance of my being here is of the utmost. So here I am."

"Marion Lightborn," she said, and she caught how Thren's eyes sparkled at the name. "I'm here with Kyle Garland."

———

41

"Such a shame," said Thren. "I was hoping you'd come alone."

"Don't fret," she told him. "Pretty blue eyes like yours, you should find many women eager to vanish into one of Maynard's rooms for a quick, private conversation."

Thren chuckled.

"I could take one of those women as easily as I take this seat. But it's not the seat I want, remember?"

Despite herself, she blushed.

"Indeed," she said.

Thren looked over his shoulder, scanning the surrounding groups that chatted nearby. Their voices were like a buzz amid the music, which sadly was not loud enough to drown them out.

"Is that him?" Thren asked, gesturing toward a pack of six. Marion sipped her glass of wine.

"That it is," she said. "The one in white, dark hair, gold on the cuffs. Such a *fine* dresser, my date."

"The devotion you show your lover is one bards would sing of for years, should they ever spend time in your presence."

Marion laughed.

"He is not my lover. I am willing to do much for wealth, but not that. Not him."

Thren leaned toward her, and his smile widened at that.

"You impress me more and more," he said.

"You give me too much credit. I'm still a whore. I'm just more selective about it is all. Besides, so far I've been given weeks of fine food, drink, and clothes to wear, and I haven't had to spread my legs once. All I've had to do is *promise* to spread my legs come a day that is always soon, always just on the horizon."

"That gem on his finger," he said. "Is that the Heart?"

Marion finished her drink.

"Kyle's pride and joy. The Heart of Ker, supposedly dug from the sands not long after the black spire crumbled and the sands were swallowed by the grasslands. Yes, that's it. He keeps it with him always. The only things that stay closer to him is his bodyguards."

"Bodyguards?"

Marion searched, gestured to one of them lurking along the wall.

"The women in the white masks." She turned back, shook her head. "I wish you could see them sparring sometime. If they weren't fucking Kyle every night, I wouldn't think they were human."

Thren let out another chuckle, and he rose from his seat.

"I think your lover has spotted me," he said, bowing low. As he did, Kyle strode over, an unpleasant look on his face.

"Marion, my dear," he said, kissing her cheek. His eyes never left Thren's face. "I see you have made a new friend."

Thren grinned.

"I wouldn't call me a friend," he said. "Good day, Lord Garland. Oh, and nice ring. Wouldn't mind having one like that for myself."

He sauntered off, as if amused by Kyle's jealous reaction. Kyle slipped into the other seat, still glaring at Thren's back.

"Who was that man?" he asked.

Marion let a small smile spread on her lips.

"He said his name was Thren."

The blood drained from Kyle's face. Up from his chair he bolted, forcefully grabbing her hand as he stared into the crowd.

"Thren?" he hissed. "As in Thren *Felhorn*?"

"Perhaps, why?"

Kyle looked down at his ring, then clenched the hand into a fist.

"That man's the Darkhand's apprentice," Kyle said, craning his neck. "He's robbed several of my caravans already, and...damn it, I can't see him anymore!"

His two bodyguards, who'd been lurking against the side of the mansion so their master could bargain and banter in privacy, saw his distress and hurried over.

"What is the matter?" asked Green.

"Thren's here," said Kyle.

"Bertram let him in?" asked Brown.

"Or he climbed the wall," said Green.

"It doesn't matter," Kyle said. "We have to leave, now. He made his intentions quite clear. He wants my ring. He wants the Heart of Ker!"

"Calm down," Marion said, pulling her hand free of his. "You don't know that. He just said it was a nice ring. Even if that was Thren, and he's here to rob people, there's hundreds here whose purses he might take instead."

"He was *mocking* me, you stupid woman," Kyle said. "What do we do, what do we do?"

"We should leave," Green said.

"There are two days left, I can't leave yet," Kyle said. "Safe, we have to get somewhere safe until I can talk to Bertram in private, let that idiot know his security isn't doing its damn job."

"To your room then," said Brown.

Marion was more dragged than led through the party toward the main entrance of the mansion. The doors were propped open, and inside the halls she saw plenty more people scurrying about. Stairs immediately before her led to the higher floor, and Kyle took them without hesitating. At the top, an older man and his wife were coming down. Kyle paused for a moment to smile and intrude into their conversation.

"Bartholomew, old friend," said Kyle. "Forgive my hurry, but I'd love to talk later. Tell me, which room is yours so I may visit when things calm down later tonight?"

"First on your left once you reach the end of the hall," said the gray-haired man. "And try not to come too late. Once these old bones get a bit of alcohol into them, sleep doesn't lurk far behind."

Kyle laughed, and Marion did her best to put on a pleasing face.

"Come on," Kyle said once they were past. Down the hall they walked, then turned left. At the first in a sea of doors they stopped, and Kyle checked the knob.

"Locked," he said, stepping aside so one of his bodyguards could slide forward. She pulled two thin wires from her pocket and, kneeling down, inserted both into the lock.

"We're breaking into the old man's room?" Marion asked, raising an eyebrow.

"I'd rather think of it as switching rooms until I can be assured of my safety," Kyle said.

With a click the lock tumbled, and the bodyguard pushed open the door. Together they stepped into a well-furnished room, the grand bed covered with seemingly endless number of blankets, great curtains furled before two large windows. Marion wrinkled her nose as behind her Green shut the door and relocked it.

"Smells like…something," she said. "Like dusty clothes in a dustier closet."

"For once will you stop complaining!" Kyle yelled, whirling on her. Marion took a step back, and she averted her gaze.

"I'm sorry," she mumbled. "I fear I erred in talking to Thren and put us all in danger. Please forgive me."

When he said nothing she took a step forward and kissed his cheek.

"Very sorry," she whispered.

Kyle cleared his throat, looked to his bodyguards.

"Thren'll come back when it's dark," he said. "Either that, or try to strike now while there's so many people milling about. We'll hunker down here until morning, then find Bertram."

"I could go now," Green said. "Thren is but a young fool. We do not need two of us to protect you from him."

"No," Kyle said as Marion slipped from his arms and walked to the window. "No, I will not leave myself vulnerable for even a second."

Marion undid the latch holding the windows shut and then pushed them open. A sudden gust of warm air blew against her, and she let out a sigh as it teased her hair.

"Much better," she said.

She thought Kyle might protest, and she heard him turn at the sound of the opening window, but he was given no time. Her eyes drifted upward, and hanging from the roof not two rooms over, with a smile on his face, was Thren Felhorn.

"He's here!" she screamed, suddenly flinging herself back from the window.

"Who? Where?" asked Kyle.

"On the roof!" Marion said, calming herself down so her next words came out only urgently instead of in an undignified screech.

"Then let us abandon hiding," Brown said, drawing one of her daggers. "I'll bring you his head, my master."

"Wait!" Kyle cried, but she ignored him. The bodyguard put a foot on the windowsill, spun, and then leaped to the rooftop, grabbing hold and pulling herself beyond Marion's line of sight. Now trembling, Marion clutched Kyle's arm to her, pressing her body against his.

"He won't kill us, will he?" she asked. "He just wants the Heart, he won't kill us, he doesn't need to kill us…"

At the door came a single solitary knock. The force of it made the hinges rattle.

"Lord Garland?" asked a deep voice. "That you in there, Kyle?"

Green put herself between the two of them and the door, and she drew her blades.

"Stay behind me," she said. "I will keep you both safe."

The door suddenly burst open, and Marion let out a soft gasp as she took a step backward. Standing there was an enormous man with dark skin and a shaved head. Several hoop earrings dangled from his ear. At his hips were buckled two swords.

"Stay…stay back," Kyle said, trying not to sound terrified. "I'll have no bloodshed here!"

The man tilted his head, and he smirked at the bodyguard, who remained crouched in a defensive stance, clearly expecting him to attack.

"Bloodshed?" asked the man. "Why, how rude. I'm not here for bloodshed."

Kyle licked his lips.

"Then what are you here for?"

The man gestured past him, toward Marion.

"I just came here to say hello to my sister, that's all."

And then he was gone, as was Marion, already diving out the open window to the room, using the rope left for her by Thren to guide her to the ground.. Once on her feet, she brushed off her dress, lifted the Heart of Ker up so

Kyle could see it clearly, and then hid it in the ample cleavage her dress created. Smiling, she blew him a kiss.

Kyle started to curse, but he pulled back into the room with a cowardly yell as the body of Green fell mere inches from his head, crumpling dead at Marion's feet.

Marion was gone long before the crowds could gather at the sight of the mangled corpse and wonder what was going on.

*

Thren sat in one of two wooden chairs in his meager apartment, legs crossed, the Heart of Ker raised high so the light from the window could set it to sparkling.

"Honestly thought it'd be tougher than that," said Grayson, plopping into the chair opposite him. His friend grinned, and he reached out for the Heart. Thren tossed it over to him, let the dark-skinned man twirl the enormous ruby in his fingers.

"You underestimate our training," Thren said, leaning his head on his fist.

"And my womanly persuasions," said Marion, coming in from the other room. She'd washed her face clean of all the powders and pampering she'd received, and instead of a red dress she now wore a tightly fitted pair of pants and a cotton shirt.

"My dear," Thren said, smiling at her, "I doubt I will ever underestimate *your* womanly persuasions."

Marion kissed her brother on the cheek even as he delivered a subtle glare Thren's way.

"I'll snag us something to eat," she said, heading to the door. "After such a score, I think all three of us deserve to celebrate."

The door shut, and as it did, Grayson tossed back the ring.

"You know what happens next," he said. "The Darkhand's going to send us east. Our training's over, and it's time we prove our worth. I think he's had his eye on Veldaren for a while now, truth be told."

Thren held the ring up once more, then put it into his pocket.

"Honestly, it's about time," he said. "We'll go to Veldaren, find ourselves a thief guild worthy of our talents. Won't be too long before we make the city ours."

Grayson laughed.

"Such confidence! Such gall! Is there ever a moment of doubt in your blond head?"

Thren looked to the door, thinking of Marion's exit.

"Not often," he said. "So, will your sister be coming with us to Veldaren?"

Grayson sensed his true line of thought, and he leaned forward in his chair.

"You're my friend," he said, "so I'll give you this warning free. Marion's off limits. If you take one more long look at my sister, touch her, kiss her, even get dirty ideas in your head just *thinking* about her, I will take my swords and shove them so far down your throat you'll be shitting steel. Just so you know."

Thren rose from his seat, and he lifted open palms to show his surrender.

"You've made your point," he said as he headed to the door and opened it.

"Where are you going?" Grayson asked.

"None of your business," Thren said, stepping out. Halfway through he paused, ducked his head back into the room. "Oh, and just so *you* know, I plan on marrying her one day."

He shut the door behind him, breathed in the fresh morning air, and laughed as he ran down the street toward the market.

Stealing Crowns

Thren Felhorn perched atop the stone gargoyle and waited for the signal from his guildmaster to start the killing. The night was dark, thick clouds spread across the sky blotting out the stars. Below him the street was quiet but for a lone wagon rattling toward them from afar, a few crates in the back covered with a dirty blanket. The driver looked tired, his shoulders slouched, but Thren knew it was an act. It was the man's head that gave it away, the way he was always shifting his face from side to side in search of ambushers.

He wasn't looking high enough.

"This is it," Grayson muttered beside him, using the gargoyle's spread wings to hide his large form. "Where's the damn signal?"

"Jorry will want to know for certain before we act," Thren said. "Now keep your voice down."

Grayson grinned at him, all dark skin and white teeth.

"Why? Scared he'll hear us? The moment he hears us is the moment he's too close to get away."

"Trust me, the Wolf Guild did not let them travel unguarded," Thren said, watching the wagon's approach. Despite his words, he saw no guards, no patrols from the rival guild. Something about it felt off. Their guildmaster, Jorry the Swift, had received word of the Wolf Guild's attempting to smuggle across town a large supply of expensive wine it had previously stolen from Lord Leon Connington. Leon, gluttonous bastard that he was, had come down hard in search of his precious wine, and the Wolf Guild was reeling from the sudden assault of mercenaries.

"Where are the guards, then?" Grayson asked, mirroring Thren's own worries. "Perhaps they can't spare anyone to watch the wagon?"

"If they get that wine out of the city and shipped west, it'll be worth a fortune in Mordan," Thren whispered. "They can spare someone. The question is where? And why hasn't Jorry sent us in to find out?"

Thren and Grayson perched on the rooftop of what had once been a temple to the priests of Karak, before they'd been chased out and the building set aflame. The stone walls remained strong and tall, a perfect vantage point for the long street below. Around the neck of the gargoyle was a rope, the length of it spooled beside Thren. Once Jorry confirmed the wagon was run by the Wolf Guild, they were to climb down and ambush it just as it passed beneath. Jorry and three others were to harass from the front, distracting the Wolves from their descent. Except the wagon was almost directly beneath them, and still Jorry had not stepped out from the side alley, signaling the start of the ambush.

"Jorry must think it's a trap," Thren said.

"As if it'd matter," Grayson said, finally whispering given the wagon's proximity. "He think we can't handle a few Wolves?"

Down the road, out stepped Jorry, his body shrouded in a deep-gray cloak, his face hidden in the darkness of the starless night. Seeing him, Thren shook his head.

"About bloody time."

He grabbed the rope and tossed it off the side of the wall. Looping it twice around his wrist, he leaped off, descending at a reckless speed. The wagon was beneath him, the rope hanging several feet above the driver's head. Into the cart's center Thren fell, his feet landing hard atop one of the crates. Before the driver could even let out a word, Thren was in the front seat, his short swords drawn, their tips pressed against the driver's throat.

"Now's not a time to make noise," Thren told him as Grayson dropped into the wagon with a thud. The lone donkey pulling the cart came to a stop as the driver pulled on the reins.

"I got nothing you'd be interested in," said the driver. He was a young man with hardly any meat hanging on his bones. "Just some flour that needs delivering before the ovens fire up in the morning."

"Flour, eh?" Grayson asked from behind him. "Care if I open up one of these to take a look?"

The driver started to look back, then stopped at Thren's glare.

"Go ahead," he said. "That flour ain't worth my life."

As Grayson bent down, Thren dared a look up the alley. Jorry was nowhere to be found. It put a rock into Thren's stomach, a certainty that things moved beyond his understanding, and he didn't like it. Before Grayson could get one of the crates open, a call sounded from the direction in which the wagon had come. The driver tensed, and Thren spared another look.

Running down the road, their armor rattling, were a half dozen armed mercenaries.

The driver's eyes were wide with terror when he saw Thren's glare.

"I didn't—" he started to say, but Thren struck the side of the man's head with the pommel of his sword, knocking him out. As the body collapsed, Thren shoved him out of the driver's seat and reached for the reins.

"No time," Grayson said, hopping out of the wagon with his two short swords drawn. "Get your ass over here, Thren."

Thren swore, then drew his own two blades. As the six men came running, Thren spared a glance, only to confirm to himself that Jorry had left them to die.

You idiot, thought Thren. *You're about to be sorely disappointed.*

With just two against six, the mercenaries clearly were not expecting a fight.

"Stay where you are," one of them commanded as the others drew their swords. Thren stood beside Grayson, each settling into a combat stance, letting their gray cloaks fall across their bodies to hide the positioning of their arms and legs.

"This business does not concern you," Thren said, taking a small step to his left to give Grayson more room to maneuver when the fight began. "Go on back to whoever pays for the privilege to hold your leash."

"By the authority of Lord Leon Connington, we demand you turn over that wagon for inspection," said the mercenaries' leader, seemingly unbothered by Thren's comment.

"Is that so?" asked Grayson. "And if we don't?"

The man opened his mouth, no doubt to issue a threat, but he had no chance to give it. Thren lunged, extending his arm to the fullest. The tip of his short sword slipped into the flesh of the man's throat, not far, just enough to leave a slender gap when Thren pulled back. Just enough to leave him gagging on his own blood.

Grayson exploded into motion so that when Thren fell back, the giant man was assaulting the right side of their group, his swords hammering against swords flung up in desperate defenses. Thren faked a run at the other three on the left, then dove right, stabbing in the back one soldier who'd turned to face Grayson. Together they finished off a third before the mercenaries could even gain their bearings. Now that it was just two on three, Thren grinned and beckoned the men closer.

"I'm still waiting," he told them. "What happens if we refuse?"

The three rushed forward in a unified charge, trusting their sharpened blades and expensive armor to protect them. If not for his anger at Jorry, Thren would have laughed. Despite their cloaks, their lack of armor, he and Grayson were no normal thugs. They'd undergone training even the mercenaries would have been appalled to witness. Thren took the two on the left, let Grayson have the third on the right. The men struck simultaneously, high chops with their long blades. Thren sidestepped one, blocked the other with the sword in his left hand. His right he swung in a circle while taking another step left. The hit knocked the soldier's blade far out of position, and Thren hopped forward, cutting the mercenary's throat.

Armor rattled as the corpse hit the ground. Thren's final opponent tried to rush him, but he stumbled over the body, which stole power from his thrust. Thren smashed aside the attack, weaving his blades into a dizzying display he knew few could follow. The mercenary tried. The mercenary failed.

"Gods damn it," Thren said as he cleaned the blood off his blades. Grayson stood amid the bodies, neck craned as he scanned down the street.

"Don't see any more coming yet," he said. "But it won't take long before more do. We need to get out of here, now."

"Indeed," Thren said.

They climbed into the wagon, with Grayson taking the reins, and driving it to their guildhouse. Two men stood outside it, and they tipped their heads at Thren and Grayson's arrival.

"What you got there?" asked one of them. "Something fancy for us to drink?"

Thren hopped down, ignoring him. He meant to barge inside, to demand to speak with Jorry, but instead the door opened and out stepped the master of the Spider Guild. Jorry was a tall man, but his body was long and lanky, his hands in particular. With a face looking just as stretched, Jorry smiled at the two.

"What took you so long to return?" he asked.

"We had a few mercenaries to kill," Thren said, struggling to contain his anger. "Mercenaries we could have used help in taking down."

"Leon's mercenaries?" asked Jorry, making a grand show of his confusion. "I saw them coming, and it's why I called off the hit. Why did you not run when they arrived?"

"Running meant leaving the wagon behind," said Grayson as more members of the Spider Guild filtered through the door, heading toward the wagon. "And unlike you, me and Thren aren't scared of a little scruff when we make a hit."

Still Jorry was smiling. Thren didn't like it one bit. Again he knew he was missing something, and when others of his guild pulled open the crates of the wagon, he realized what it was.

"Flour?" asked one. "What the shit we going to do with this, bake ourselves a cake?"

Thren felt his neck flush red as others began to laugh.

"Get it into the guildhouse," Jorry ordered. "We'll find ourselves a use for Thren's grand score tonight somehow."

———

Despite their having gathered in the middle of the street, leaving themselves open to ambush or spying, Thren's hand drifted to the hilt of his sword. His blue eyes met Jorry's brown, and within them he saw the dark amusement twinkling.

"You gave us the signal," Thren said quietly.

"I stepped out to usher you home," Jorry said. "Our informant was wrong. Ah well. Good thing you didn't get hurt fighting those mercenaries."

The guildmaster turned and, laughing, strode back into the guildhouse.

Grayson's hand fell atop Thren's shoulder, but Thren shook it off.

"He got us," Grayson said as the rest of the wagon was unloaded, leaving the two alone. "No shame in that. Jorry's a clever one. That's how he got where he is, after all."

"He wanted us dead," Thren said.

"And we want him dead. It's only fair."

Thren shook his head.

"In that, it is only politics and power. This was mockery. I won't have it, not with our reputation yet to be established here in Veldaren. I won't let us become known as the flour thieves."

Grayson shrugged.

"It's got a unique ring to it."

His friend was just trying to maintain his humor, especially after such a mess-up, but Thren knew he couldn't risk such a stain remaining on his reputation.

"No, Grayson," he said. "It's time we took over the Spider Guild."

Grayson laughed.

"And how will we do that?"

In answer, Thren kicked open the door to the guildhouse and marched inside. Once beyond the guarded entryway he stepped into the building's wide single floor lit by dozens of candles and filled with members of the Spider Guild, by far the most dangerous and prosperous of Veldaren's many thief guilds. Its various members were busy drinking and chatting with the women who would be sharing their beds that night. In the far corner Thren spotted Jorry, a woman at either side of him and a drink in the hand not busy groping their thighs.

"Thren!" shouted Jorry, seeing him enter. "Come to join me?"

In answer, Thren took out his sword and smashed it onto the center of a round table before him. The two men drinking at it looked up at him in shock, then quickly backed away. The brown drink from their spilled glasses dripped down to the floor.

"You've insulted me," Thren said in the suddenly still room. "I don't forgive insults, not lightly."

Jorry leaned forward, and he sipped from his glass before setting it aside.

"What is it you *want*, Thren?" he asked. "It's my position, isn't it? You've been in my guild less than a year, yet you still eye my power. I'd call you arrogant, but it doesn't come near far enough. I know you're skilled with a sword, but that just makes you a killer. Last I remember, we're a *thieves* guild, not sellswords."

"And I am the better thief," Thren said.

"A bold claim," Jorry said. "But you're talking to Jorry the Swift. How do you think I obtained such a title?"

"I always assumed it was from your time with the ladies," Grayson said, striding in from the street and coming to Thren's side. He crossed his arms, putting his fingers within easy reach of the hilts of his swords.

58

"So funny, so clever," Jorry said, slowly rising to his feet. All around him Thren saw members of the Spider Guild reaching for their daggers and swords. There were over fifty crammed into that room, not counting the whores. Even if he could kill Jorry, there would be no guild for him to rule. They'd string him up and then bleed him out in the most creative ways they could imagine. But Thren wasn't interested in killing Jorry. Well, not yet, anyway.

"I'm done with you," said Jorry. "Your ego, your stubbornness. Whatever usefulness you've known has long passed."

"You want me gone?" Thren asked. "A challenge, then. A chance for you to prove your superiority."

Jorry tilted his head, his expression carefully guarded.

"Is that so? And why should I accept?"

"You're the better thief," said Thren. "Or will you cower before your own guild?"

Jorry chuckled, and he reached for his drink.

"So be it," he said. "What is your challenge?"

Thren knew it had to be worthy, something the entire guild would remember should either he or Jorry be successful. Something the guildmaster's pride would never let him turn down.

"A simple theft," he said. "The first to retrieve the king's crown wins."

The silence around them quickly turned to a roar. Jorry laughed, as if taken aback by Thren's audacity.

"The king's crown it is!" he cried. "And what do I get if I win?"

"If you win, Grayson and I will toss aside our cloaks, and my family and I will never step foot in Veldaren again."

"Be still my heart," said Jorry. "And if you win?"

———

Thren shrugged.

"You step down as guildmaster, and acknowledge me the better thief. Let us swear it now, with our entire guild as witness."

Their gazes met again, and Thren knew he had him. The risk was great, but Jorry knew that if it came to a clash of swords, there would be no victory for him. But in nighttime acquisitions? There were very few better than Jorry, and honestly, Thren did not consider himself one of them. But in this he'd have to be.

"I accept," Jorry said, lifting his glass in a toast. "Let the contest begin!"

*

The following night Thren and Grayson leaned against the front of a closed shop and stared up the road leading to King Gregor Vaelor's castle.

"I'm not sure why I have to come with you," Grayson said.

"Because you're banished along with me if I fail."

"That is sort of my point."

Thren grinned at his friend.

"You know you'd come with me on this even if I tried to stop you, so stop complaining. Besides, we have a castle to break into."

"Speaking of," said Grayson, gesturing to the distant edifice. "How exactly will we be going about doing just that?"

"Castles are made to hold off armies," Thren said. "Against two men…well, that's a different matter. Follow me, and I'll show you a door no one ever remembers."

Thren ran toward the eastern side of the castle, barely able to hear Grayson's muttered complaint.

"Cocky bastard…"

There were no walls to protect the castle and its adjoining prison; for the longest time the wall surrounding the city of Veldaren had been enough. Instead the castle relied upon its thick doors and constant patrols, and neither felt insurmountable to Thren. Keeping just beyond sight of the patrols, Thren led Grayson to the far side, where the castle jutted up against the great wall. More soldiers walked along the top, well armed and carrying torches. In the shadow of that wall they approached the castle.

"So what exactly are we looking for?" Grayson whispered into his ear as Thren paused for a moment to wait for another patrol to meander by.

"I said a door," Thren whispered back. "Have some faith."

A foul smell grew steadily worse the closer to the castle they came, until Thren could barely stand it, and Grayson was cursing him under his breath. They were just to where the castle joined with the wall, and in the crevice they formed the ground was soft and reeked of filth. No torches shone on them there, for which Thren was thankful. Remaining hidden would have been difficult given how distracted he was. With the best dramatic reveal he could pull off with one hand covering his nose, he gestured to his entrance.

"No," Grayson whispered. "No, no, and above all, fuck no."

The various sewer pipes in the castle all led to one large drainage exit, an open chute that ran from the castle to the wall. That chute dumped the piss and shit into a sharply slanted hole halfway up the wall, allowing it to slide out of the city.

"We've dealt with worse," Thren whispered as he removed his shoes and stuffed them into a pocket of his shirt. "Now get your shoes off. We need them clean if we're to sneak through the castle without leaving a trail for all the world to see."

Again Grayson shook his head.

"You're like my brother," he said, "but I'm not crawling through that. I'd rather be banished to the farthest corner of the world."

"If you say so."

Taking a deep breath, Thren climbed his way up the wall, finding easy handholds in the worn stone. Upon reaching the chute, he grabbed the side. The metal was sharp, and he winced, glad that it only dug into his skin instead of cutting it. The wince was also for the sludge his fingers dug into, and he was beyond thankful that it was dark, and he would see very little of what he was about to crawl through. Hoisting himself up, he slid into the chute once another patrol had passed, and that done, he put down elbow after elbow as he made his way up the castle's asshole.

Claustrophobia set in only once, after about five minutes of worming his way through. The chute was slick, which prevented him from getting stuck, but the smell was overwhelming, and worse was how he had to keep his head low to it due to the cramped space. Slowly he breathed in and out, pushing away the maddening certainty in his head that the walls were closing in on him. As he did, he heard motion behind him, followed by a gagged whisper.

"Move it, Thren, or I'm pushing my way past. Not staying in here a second longer than I have to."

Thren smiled, and the last of his claustrophobia passed. Elbow after elbow, until he reached the initial opening of the sewage chute. No doubt the room was actually dark, with only a little light filtering in through the crack beneath its door, but to Thren it was a shining, glorious paradise. Putting his bare feet on the cold stone, he wiped them as best he could before putting on his shoes. After that he stripped to his bare chest, hurling the rest of his outfit back into the sewage hole. Grayson did the same.

"Ready?" Thren asked, checking the lone short sword tightly strapped to his thigh. Thankfully the scabbard had protected the blade from the filth.

"You owe me forever," Grayson said, taking a moment to gather himself, breathing heavily with his back to their entrance. "And yes, ready."

Thren had learned everything he could about the layout of the castle from the few members of the Spider Guild who had been inside. From what he knew, the crown would be kept in the royal treasury, which was on the lowest floor. They themselves were on the second floor, reserved mostly for the servants' quarters and to house the castle guard. Not the best place to be, but the night was deep, and the soldiers who were awake were busy manning the walls or protecting the king and queen's bedchambers, as well as their son, Edwin.

Exiting the room, they hurried down the hall after a brief moment to confirm their location. To their right was a long corridor with many doors, which Thren guessed to be bedrooms. The other way led to the stairs, and down these they went. At the very bottom waited two soldiers, their backs to them. Thren motioned to the left, and Grayson nodded. Not a noise made by their steps, the two attacked together, simultaneously cutting the soldiers' throats before they could let out a single cry. That done, they sheathed their blades, hooked a right, and rushed as fast as they could down the quiet hall.

"No hesitation," Thren whispered as they neared a corner, around which he expected to find the treasury.

No stealth this time; instead they ran about with weapons drawn...only to find two soldiers laying facedown before an open door, twin pools of blood spreading beneath their necks. Stepping inside, Thren glanced around, and wasn't surprised by what he saw.

"Well shit," Grayson said, and Thren couldn't help but laugh given how their night had gone.

"There's a reason he's called the Swift," Thren said.

The crown was gone, and despite the many bars of gold around him, Thren was sure a few of those were gone as well. Jorry had beaten them there.

"What do we do now?" Grayson asked. "A few bars of gold will help ease the pain, at least make it worthwhile to suffer through that damn shithole again."

Thren turned, put a dirty hand on his friend's shoulder.

"I knew he'd beat us," he said. "I had to see for certain, just in case. But it looks like it'll be the hard path after all."

"The hard path?" asked Grayson.

At that, Thren only smiled.

*

After cleaning up, Thren and Grayson returned to the guildhouse, which was in the middle of a celebration even more raucous than the night before. In the center of them all stood Jorry, accepting their adulation with a grin on his face that spread from ear to ear. Atop his head was King Gregor's crown, the inset gems glittering in the candlelight.

"So you return, and just in time!" Jorry cried upon their arrival.

Thren stepped closer to his guildmaster as Grayson remained by the door, a large sack slung over his shoulder.

"I see you have a crown," Thren said, keeping his face passive.

"Not just *a* crown," said Jorry. "*The* crown. I am the Swift, Thren, the unstoppable Spider."

The man continued, his speech clearly for the audience and not for Thren.

"I slipped past every soldier on patrol, some mere feet away when I sneaked behind their backs. In the halls of the castle I kept to every shadow. A servant was more likely to hear a cockroach's fart than to hear my passing. The treasury was locked and barred, with several guards on watch. Subduing the guards was child's play, a diversion here, a sound there, all to get near enough for my dagger to do its work. Even the lock, perhaps the finest-built in the entire nation, was but a plaything to me. And with the crown in hand, and a coiled rope on my back, I climbed one of the nearby towers. From its window I scaled down, all before a single alarm could be sounded."

Jorry lifted the crown from his head, held it before him, and then set it down on a table to his left. The whole while Thren had stood with his arms crossed, merely waiting for the spiel to end.

"So," said Jorry, finally bringing his attention back to Thren. "It'll be such a shame that a pretty lass like Marion'll have to leave us, but perhaps she'll be smart enough to stay here instead of leaving with an arrogant prick like you. By the Abyss, even your son's welcome to remain behind. I could always use a new servant, maybe teach him how to be an excellent thief, unlike his father."

Jorry sneered, then gestured to Grayson.

"Well, let's make this official. What did you get from your little jaunt into the castle? Did you take a few of the candleholders and silverware I left behind?"

Thren looked back to Grayson, nodded.

———

"Not quite," he said.

The giant man tossed the bag toward Jorry. It hit the ground with a plop, and the loosely tied string along the top twisted open. Out from the bag rolled two heads, one male, one female. The room turned deathly quiet as all there recognized them for who they were.

The king and queen.

Thren walked over to the king's head and picked it up by the hair. The sound of his drawing his blade was deafening in the silence. Slowly he cut across the king's scalp, slicing until the head fell back to the ground. That done, Thren sheathed his sword, then walked over to the table on which Jorry had placed his own trophy.

"The king's crown," Thren said, dropping the piece of hair and flesh next to it. Slowly he turned, addressing all there.

"A crown of gold, or a crown of flesh. Which will you all choose? Do you want petty baubles, or do you want to make kingdoms tremble?"

His rotation complete, he fixed his gaze on Jorry, who looked ready to explode with rage.

"You are an excellent thief," Thren told him. "But I am the true master here. Step down and serve me. There is much good you can still do for the Spider Guild."

Jorry shook his head.

"You're a liar and a cheat," he said.

Thren smiled.

"Who better to rule a guild of thieves?"

In a single smooth motion he stepped forward, drew out his sword, and plunged it into Jorry's belly. As the man doubled over, Thren yanked free his blade, twirled, and then decapitated his former guildmaster. The body collapsed amid a cacophony of shouts, accusations, and questions. Putting his back to a wall, Thren stared at them, he on one side of the building, Grayson blocking the door on the other.

"The Spider Guild is mine," Thren said to them. "You may leave, or you may stay. For those of you who are loyal, to every one of you, I promise a golden crown."

To each one he looked, unflinching, letting them see the coldness in his eyes.

"And if you would challenge me, if you would deny my rule, then step forward now. Speak your name, show your face."

He gestured to the bloody mass on the table.

"To you," he said, "I also promise a crown."

And then he sheathed his sword, crossed his arms, and waited. The men looked to one another, and then a man grabbed the nearest drink, despite its not being his, and lifted it into the air.

"To our new guildmaster!" he cried, just the first of many. "Slayer of kings, and master of Spiders!"

Slayer of kings, thought Thren, and seeing Grayson laughing by the door, he smiled. The guild was his now, to shape and mold into something far greater than it already was. Muzien had sent them east to form a reputation, to prove all their training and education had been worthwhile.

Slayer of kings.

It was a good start.

Stealing Life

For once Thren wished he'd left the wealthy Maynard Gemcroft alone instead of ambushing the man's latest shipment of minted coins from his mines in Tyneham. Thren's task that night would have been far easier, and its reward was worth far more than any fortune.

"Coming with?" Thren asked Grayson as he strapped his swords to his side.

"I can't leave," Grayson said. "You know that. I have to be here, just in case."

Thren nodded.

"I understand."

With that he crept open the door to the meager home they hid within, ensured no soldiers lurked nearby, and then dashed out. As fast as his legs could carry him, Thren ran down the road, his gray cloak billowing behind him. He thought to take it off, decided against it. If he was without the cloak, members of other guilds might think him a potential target. With it, though...with it he was leader of the Spider Guild, and only a fool would dare draw a blade against him.

Maynard's mercenaries, on the other hand, were quite foolish.

"Down here!" cried a small squad, rounding the corner behind him before Thren realized they were there. "On Cale, running on Cale!"

———

Shit, thought Thren as he dove to the side, avoiding a hastily shot arrow. Getting off Cale Road was first priority, second being to escape the enclosing net of armored men that was converging on him. Never before had any member of the wealthy Trifect mustered so many mercenaries to hunt for him. His score must have bothered Maynard more than Thren had expected. Shallow compensation.

He hooked a right at the first alley he found, but instead of running toward its end he jumped left, grabbed a windowsill on the second floor, and used it to haul himself up to the roof. There he rolled onto his back, catching his breath as the soldiers ran on without realizing where he'd gone. Sharp pieces of rock bit into the back of his head and neck, and he brushed the gravel from beneath him.

No time, thought Thren. *No time for any of this, gods damn it!*

Back on his feet, despite hearing soldiers nearby calling out to the other patrols. Back on his feet, legs pumping, heart pounding in his chest. He leaped from building to building, hardly pausing to see if any below would notice. Taking as straight a line as he could, he made his way toward his destination: the temple to Ashhur. He could see it in the distance, a white marble structure lit with thick torches along the front. There was a wide expanse before the stairs, which worried Thren immensely.

That worry was confirmed when he stopped at the edge of a roof, crouching down to peer in each direction. The mercenaries, at least a hundred now by his count, were systematically spreading out in hopes of spotting him again. Along the road between him and the temple walked one group, moving far too slowly for Thren's taste. The temple was right there, taunting him, but to cross meant being spotted.

So be it. He hung down from the rooftop, then released. When he hit the ground he rolled to absorb the blow, then came up with his weapons drawn. He'd not wait for them to pass, not given what was at stake, so instead he rushed the three head on, with but the rustle of his cloak to give them warning. They carried torches, and the light blinded them to the darkness beyond, and it was from that darkness he rushed.

One short sword took out the closest man, piercing through the gap between his helmet and shoulder pauldron. His second struck the torch out of the frontmost mercenary's hand. The sudden shift in light was all the advantage he needed, coupled with the surprise. With unmatched ferocity he lunged at the remaining two, stabbing another through the stomach. The man started to let out a scream, but Thren sliced out his throat before he could. The third did yell for aid, but couldn't get his voice to carry, for he was too busy falling back, flailing to put his sword among Thren's constant barrage of thrusts.

Three times Thren swung both his blades simultaneously, smashing them into the mercenary's defense. The fourth time he feinted, pulling his foe's weapon out of position. Stepping closer, he kicked the man's knee, dropping him. In went his short swords, thrusting through his neck as he let out a gargled death cry. In a crumple of armor the man fell, the sound horribly loud to Thren's ears. He glanced up and down the street, but he saw no one, and could only hope that he might be in and out of the temple before anyone stumbled upon the bodies.

Thren knew he shouldn't be surprised the temple door was unlocked, but he was anyway. Not because the priests who professed mercy and forgiveness were actually so trusting. More because the way his night was going, he felt as if a thousand pounds of iron chains should have prevented his entrance. Perhaps, just perhaps, things might still turn out well.

Immediately upon entrance he stepped into a long carpeted hallway leading into a room of worship. It was filled with rows of pews, hard wood with little padding. There were doors on both the left and the right of the far side, and as he ran across the carpet he wondered which way might lead to where the priests slept. Guessing left, he went to the door, checked it. Unlocked as well, and through it he went.

Beyond was a hallway lit with long candles. Unsure of what to do, he picked a door at random and checked it. Like the others, it was unlocked. Carefully he turned the knob, pushed it open, and then stepped through. Inside was a small room with a small desk and a small cot. Upon that cot slept a middle-aged man. Thren drew a sword, then knelt down and put a hand across the man's mouth. Immediately the man's eyes opened. To Thren's surprise, he showed no sign of panic despite his predicament.

"Not a sound," Thren whispered. "When I remove my hand, you will tell me your name."

"Calan," was his response when his mouth was uncovered.

"Are you a priest?" Thren asked.

Calan nodded. He seemed a harmless man, with a round nose and face, his ears big and his eyes green.

"What is it you need, son?" Calan asked, and Thren was happy the man had the intelligence to whisper his question.

"What I need," said Thren, grabbing him by the arm, "is for you to come with me."

*

He'd hoped making his way back would be easier, but the mercenaries were showing no sign of letting up.

They'd spread farther out since failing to locate him earlier, but that just meant every direction he faced led him toward some patrol or other. At least the priest made no overt attempts to escape, instead following along like a properly trained dog. Street by street Thren worked his way toward the safe house, the whole while wishing they could take to the rooftops instead.

"Hurry," he said, catching sight of torches coming just around the bend. As they cut into an alley, he swore, seeing torchlight up ahead as well. Spinning about, he realized he was caught between two groups.

"Damn it, Maynard, this isn't funny," he said, trying to decide what to do.

"Friend," said Calan as light from the torches shone their way, and they heard cries demanding they halt. "The reason you take me, is it to help someone, or hurt them?"

Thren swallowed down a heavy lump in his throat.

"Help," he said.

"Then remove your cloak, and follow."

Calan approached the mercenaries, walking with his hands out at his sides. After a moment's hesitation Thren smoothly removed the clasp about his neck and let his cloak fall to the dirt of the alley.

"Identify yourselves," said one of the men in the small squad of four. He held his torch closer, and his eyes widened as the light reflected off Thren's swords.

"My name is Calan, priest of Ashhur," said Calan. "With me is a friend who has come to me in this dark hour with great need."

The torch moved closer to Thren, until he felt the heat of it on his face.

"What's your name?" the man asked Thren.

"His name is none of your concern," Calan said before Thren could lie. "As is his business. Matters of faith and healing are matters no sellsword should interfere with. Now put down your swords, let us pass, and spend the rest of this night in peace."

Thren thought there wasn't a chance the four would do as asked, but there was a strange forcefulness to the priest's voice, a sudden firmness that seemed to contradict the smooth, harmless look of the man. And then the torch pulled away, and the squad saluted.

"Not safe out tonight," one told them as they marched away. "I'd suggest going home."

"I am," Thren said, and he looked to Calan. The priest gestured farther down the alley, to where it joined with another road.

"Lead on," he said. "I am no fool, and can sense your despair. Someone is in danger, now lead, and do not bother with hiding the way. No one will bother us further."

Thren opened his mouth, closed it, and then ran along.

They reached the safe house not long after. Thren opened the door and gestured for Calan to enter. Looking around one last time to ensure no one spotted them, Thren stepped in.

Immediately he heard the screaming, and it was a knife to his heart. Calan heard it as well, and without waiting for orders he hurried through the meagerly furnished room and through the door into the bedroom, where Marion lay.

"How long has she been like this?" Calan asked as Thren followed. Grayson stood at Marion's side, holding her hand as she cried. Marion lay on the bed, the sheets cast off to the side. At her feet was an elderly midwife, her wrinkled skin looking pale. Thren noticed she purposefully did not meet his eye when she stepped aside to make way for Calan.

"Marion's been laboring for seven hours," said the midwife. "But the bleeding, perhaps an hour. I can help the baby along, but I cannot stop the bleeding. Miracles are not my domain, priest."

"Nor are they mine," said Calan. "Only Ashhur's."

Thren went to Marion's side opposite Grayson, and he kissed his wife's cheek as she sucked in air, her screams momentarily passing as her contractions subsided.

"You'll be fine," he told her. "You're strong, stronger than anyone I know."

"Wh—" She stopped, clenched her jaw and arched her neck for a brief moment, then relaxed again. "Where's Randith?"

"Senke's watching over him," he said, stroking her face. Her hair was slick with sweat, and if he'd thought the midwife was pale, Marion seemed a ghost.

"I want to see him," she said, closing her eyes and rolling her head back. "I want to see him, please, I want to see him before…before…"

"Stop it," Thren said, refusing to let her finish. "You will see your son again, now you keep breathing, keep fighting, you hear me?"

Thren looked up, saw Grayson looking at him. Tears were in his friend's eyes.

"I'll get him," Grayson said. "If you want me to."

Thren felt something twist in his throat, and he found talking suddenly much more difficult.

"No," he said. "It's too dangerous."

Calan had exchanged words with the midwife, then shifted so she might once more have access to the baby. When Thren had left, the baby's progress had completely stopped prior to crowning, and despite his wife's constant labor, it refused to move farther down. Despite his time away, the baby had remained, and he could only imagine Marion's agony.

—

No, he didn't have to imagine it. He just had to look at the fiery woman he loved more than the world itself. Had to see the way her neck was flushed red, the way blood had spilled into her eyes from vessels bursting, feel the frantic grip with which she clutched his hand.

"Childbirth is something of which I know very little," Calan said, shifting his attention between Thren and Grayson. "But bleeding and injury, that is something else, something I'm more familiar with. Paula here will force the baby through, and then I will do what I can to keep Marion alive."

He took in a deep breath, let it out.

"I can make no promises," he said.

"Just do what you know to do," Thren said. "And waste no more time. Get on with it."

Thren had no desire to watch, his focus solely on his wife. He leaned in closer, felt the heat coming off her in waves. Gently he kissed her eyebrows, her cheek, then leaned his forehead against her as she let out a terrible scream, louder than any before. It seemed to tear out of her, going on and on.

And then it halted.

"Marion," he whispered, feeling tears running down his face. All color was gone from her now, and her eyes rolled up into her head. Her mouth hung open, her upper body shaking as if she had been struck with a deep shiver in the middle of winter. Prayers rolled from Calan's lips, an urgent stream with words that seemed to wash over Thren like water. It seemed everywhere on the bed he looked he saw blood.

When the baby let out a wail, it only shoved the knife in Thren's heart all the deeper. Stepping away from his wife, Thren looked to Grayson, saw the man standing there in shock, an ebony statue shedding tears. Thren turned more, and suddenly a bundled life was in his hands, a boy, remnants of blood still on his exposed face and arms, the skin a flushed red. The baby more mewled than cried, with far less strength than had been in the howl with which Randith let out coming into the world.

Paula the midwife stood in the corner, washing her hands with a frown on her face that told Thren everything he needed to know. Out of the room he stepped, unable to be there, unable to watch as Marion's body grew ever stiller despite the prayers of the priest.

A boy, thought Thren, staring down at the crying child as if it were this bizarre thing. *What name did we promise to use if it was a boy?*

"Aaron," he whispered, finally remembering. It was as if his mind no longer wanted to work. He kept thinking of the way Marion had convulsed in his arms, kept hearing the echo of that long, horrid shriek.

Thren stared down at Aaron. The baby's eyes were swollen shut, his nose pressed downward. Atop his head was a shock of blond hair, so much like Thren's own. So little of Marion, he realized. Would she be denied to him even in the life that had taken her away?

"Aaron," Thren whispered again, trying to evoke something in himself, to make this alien thing he held suddenly have meaning. He wanted to feel protective toward it, to feel he could sacrifice the world to ensure its safety. Upon his holding Randith, not even a king's army could have forced the baby from his arms. But what was this thing? This crying, angry thing that twitched within the blood-soaked towel?

It was a death sentence, a murderer, a thief of the life of his beloved Marion. This baby had stolen away her future, stolen away the very breath from her lungs and left her pouring out lifeblood upon a mattress. Much as Thren tried to deny it, much as he tried to remind himself that he held one of the few pieces of Marion left in the world, he felt only rage. Cold rage, something unlike what he felt when a man betrayed him, or a lord or member of the Trifect dared insult him. There was so little emotion to it, so little passion. It was angered death in him, an all-consuming thought.

"You took her from me," Thren whispered. "Why? What cruel joke in this world decided she was to die now? She'll never hold you, never feed you. Your older brother will grow, mature, take a wife of his own, and never again behold the face of his mother."

He was crying again, though he'd never realized he'd started. He noticed only when the tears fell upon Aaron's face. The baby's crying had begun to subside, still constant but not as strong. For a brief moment Thren thought the baby might die there, rendering Marion's sacrifice worthless…and the only thing he felt was satisfaction. Escape. Already the burden of raising Randith would be on his shoulders. Did he want this creature to be his as well?

All it'd take was a shift of the towel wrapped about him. So easy it'd be to block the air from his lungs. So easy to bury him along with his mother, to say goodbye to the future he should have had.

Thren's fingers grabbed the top of the towel. Thren's eyes widened, and he felt the cold rage dwindling down into emptiness, total emptiness. He no longer cared. Not about himself, not about Marion, not about Aaron. Was it shock? He didn't know. Did it matter? Higher he pulled the towel, then shifted his fingers, pressing it against Aaron's mouth. The baby's crying immediately stopped. As he held on tight, Aaron's legs kicked harder, his arms flailing out to the sides.

The door to the other room opened, and out stepped Grayson. Thren pulled back the towel, shifted his arms to hide what he'd done.

"What?" asked Thren as Aaron resumed his crying.

"Marion wants to see her baby," Grayson said, and despite his tears, a smile spread wide across his face. "Now get your ass in here."

It was as if the stone about his heart shattered. Thren felt he could breathe again, felt as if the room weren't so dark. Slowly he walked inside, Aaron cradled in his arms. Marion smiled at him from the bed, still deathly pale, but she was herself again, her bloodshot eyes showing recognition for the first time in hours. Calan stood beside her, looking very much drained.

"Praise Ashhur," he said, putting his hands on his back and stretching until it popped.

"Indeed," said Thren, feet moving of their own accord. Once at Marion's side he offered the baby to her, and she gently took him and placed his mouth to her breast.

"It's a boy," she said, her voice raspy.

"His name's Aaron," Thren said. "Randith should be happy. He's always wanted a brother to play with."

"Aaron," Marion cooed, then laid her head back on her pillow and closed her eyes. "I'm glad we picked that name. It suits him."

Thren didn't quite see how it did, but he would not question her now. His hands free, he wiped the tears from his face and tried to recover his bearings. Glancing into the other room, he almost felt as if he'd stepped out of a different world, a darkness to which he wanted never to return.

Grayson once more went to his sister's side, and with him cradling her, Calan took the time to gently pull Thren aside.

"Why did you think you must drag me here at sword's edge?" the man asked.

Thren started to answer, stopped. It seemed almost stupid now, but it was hard to explain the panic they'd all been in as Marion's health failed through the night.

"Because I feared you'd say no," he said. "Given who I am. Who we are."

Calan put a hand on his arm.

"I don't care if you're the king, a peasant, or Thren Felhorn. I'd have still come, and still done my best to save that woman's life."

Thren grinned.

"I *am* Thren Felhorn."

Calan froze for a moment, then chuckled.

"Well. It's good to know I didn't make such a boast in vain. Both those lives, your child's and your wife's, are miracles. Cherish them. Protect them. I do not know what fate awaits them, but I pray the gift was given wisely."

Thren crossed his arms and looked away. The gods weren't for him, he knew, and he felt uncomfortable with the priest's admonition.

"You're free to leave," he said.

Calan nodded, moved to the door.

"I stole a life away from the Reaper this night," the priest said as he opened it. "Look to yourself, Thren, and then to the child. Make it mean something."

And then he left.

Thren went back into the room, saw the midwife attending Marion to help with Aaron's latching, and Grayson leaning against a corner of the room with his eyes closed, fast asleep. Back to the bed he walked, and he let his eyes settle on Aaron Felhorn.

Make it mean something, echoed Calan's words in his head.

Thren didn't know how, didn't know what it even meant, but he knew that come his future days, he would ensure just that. Randith would be his elder son, heir to the empire of drugs, theft, and murder that Thren daily built. But Aaron? Aaron would be something more. Something special.

Someone to steal life from the Reaper.

Stealing Memories

Thren kissed his wife on the lips, then told her goodbye. "Don't worry," he said, pausing at the door to the quaint home on the corner of the winding street. "The Scorpion Guild will never find you here."

Marion smiled at him, exotic and beautiful despite the simple dress she wore, which clung to her dark skin and hinted at so very little being worn underneath.

"I'm more worried about not being found," she said. "Do not forget about me here, and bring my boys to me when you feel it safe. I miss them already."

She gave Thren a look he'd often wilted under before, one that promised a fiery passion should he return to her. All he had to do was momentarily escape the guilds, the dealings, the bloodshed and drugs.

"I miss *you* already as well," she told him.

Thren chuckled, shook his head, and then stepped out into the street. Waiting for him was Grayson, arms crossed over his muscular chest.

"I'm telling you," he said in his baritone voice. "It's not safe here."

"And why is that?" Thren asked as the two walked down the empty street. Worn homes were on either side of them, many with boarded windows and locked doors. The territory was newly taken by Thren and his Spider Guild, and it still showed the remnants of the bloody conflict that had earned him the victory.

"Territory's too new," Grayson insisted, rubbing a hand over his shaved head. "This was Scorpion territory for years. Those who live here, they aren't loyal to us, not yet. Too many are watching us from the cracks in their windows. I fear at least one will run to Carr, hoping to earn themselves a shiny copper."

Thren paused at the end of the street, glanced back at the home his wife hid within.

"I know," he said, turning away. "I'm expecting it."

Grayson barred the way before he could take another step.

"No," his friend said. "No, you won't do this. I won't allow it."

"She's not at risk," Thren said.

"You don't know that."

"Yes, I do."

"Damn it," Grayson said, shoving Thren back. "She's my sister!"

Before he'd even taken a staggering step back, Thren had already drawn one of his short swords and pointed it at the enormous man.

"And my wife, or have you forgotten?" he asked, meeting Grayson's hard stare. He let his voice drop. "Carr won't dare harm a hair on her head, Grayson. Not while his own wife and son are in my custody. He'll only want to take her to keep things even between us. If I can ambush him in the act, I can devastate his ranks, perhaps even capture the slimy bastard himself."

Grayson's hands flexed, hovering over his own swords before relaxing.

"How many men are watching the house?" he asked.

"A dozen, all my finest," Thren said. "I'll be here as well. The moment he makes his move, we'll be on them. I promise."

They resumed walking down the street, an act Thren knew he had to carry out before he could slink back through the darker streets to take up the watch with the rest of his men.

"You're pushing against Carr too hard," Grayson said. "You're not giving him the respect he deserves."

"I'm the best guildmaster Veldaren has ever known," Thren said. "There is no one smarter, no one better, no one more ruthless than I."

"And before you, Carr was the youngest, the fastest, the most ruthless."

Thren chuckled. Of course he knew that. For a time the man known only as Carr had been the one they'd never dared cross, even as together Thren and Grayson hopped from guild to guild, establishing their reputation in Veldaren. But that was years ago, before he'd asked Marion to marry him, promising a life and wealth far beyond the petty riches they'd known. Before he'd overthrown Jorry the Swift and claimed the Spider Guild as his own.

The riches had followed, the years had passed, and slowly the Spider Guild had grown from just another guild to something all the others watched in fear as street after street switched from Viper, or Hawk, or Crow, to the circle and lines of the Spider.

"There's a reason we've gone after Carr over the past year," Thren said as they stepped out into Iron Road, a far more populated stretch linking several smithies and tinkers' shops. "He's the one everyone was afraid of. He's the one all the other guilds must account for in their plans. This city will never view us as its rulers so long as Carr is alive. Street by street, deal by deal, we'll crush him. No one's dared challenge him, yet now I have his wife and son. He'll act rash, he'll act stupid, and he'll act afraid."

"So be it," Grayson said. "But I'm going back into the house. I won't let her stay there alone."

"She's not alone," Thren said, pushing aside a cutpurse no older than seven who had been angling too close. The brat looked baffled that he'd been noticed, and he wisely rushed away. "Wallace and Michael are in there with her. I've had them hidden inside for days now, waiting for Marion."

Grayson shook his head.

"You did all this, yet told me none of it? I'm starting to think my title as your right hand is just a way to keep me happy."

Thren smacked him on the shoulder.

"When it comes to Marion, I play everything close to the chest," he said. "Now gather up your best fighters. Make sure you bring Pennell with you. Come nightfall, I want you to assault their warehouse on Flintsteel Road. Brag long and loud about it too, especially near Pennell. He's been selling information to Carr the past few weeks."

Grayson froze in his tracks.

"Pennell?" he said. "That drunken idiot?"

"Watch him the next time he drinks," Thren said. "More ends up on his shirt than in his mouth."

The two passed through Iron, then onto the main road leading east to west through the heart of the walled city of Veldaren. With the traffic so much louder, especially due to the midday trading, the two could talk with ease.

"Why let Carr know about my attack on the warehouse?" Grayson asked.

"He'll assume the attack is the reason why we're hiding Marion," Thren said.

"And if he sets up a trap for me at the warehouse?"

Thren laughed.

"Carr will have the entire building empty before you set foot near it, just to mock me. We're playing a game, Grayson, and Carr is going to find out just how many moves behind me he actually is."

The enormous man stopped at a stand selling fruit, bought himself a few apples, and then began eating one.

"We're far enough," he said, tossing one of the apples to Thren. "Here. In case you get hungry while waiting. I don't like this, Thren, but I'm trusting you. Keep her safe, and I'll do my best to play the distraction."

Thren saluted with the apple.

"We can kill Carr at any time," he told his most trusted friend. "But it's not about the killing. It's about the message you send. When I do take his life, I want all of Veldaren's underworld to realize just how dangerous it is to cross paths with a Spider."

With that, Thren pulled his gray cloak tighter around his shoulders, then let the hood fall over his features. Into the alley he went, away from the crowds, away from the noise, and into the shadows and darkness that he had known all his life. In a world of backroom deals, of men who bought herbs and powders with stolen coin and fled from encounters with whores with shame in their eyes, Thren felt himself their king. These pitiful creatures, slaves to addictions and lusts, would always come crawling to him to feed their needs. Without need of chains or collars, Thren enslaved them all, building an empire on the backs of the weak.

But there were pretenders to his throne, and Carr was the most prominent. The Scorpion Guild had to suffer an embarrassing collapse to trigger the cannibalization that Thren desired. Let the other guilds pick apart the remains, taking territory in a mad dash to capitalize on Carr's death.

And in the chaos, they wouldn't realize that with a relentless creep, the Spiders were taking more of their own territory.

That's how you build a web, he thought. *One strand at a time.*

Directly opposite the house Marion stayed in was a burned-out husk of a building. Thren himself had set fire to it when they moved on the territory. Over ten Scorpions had been hiding inside, waiting to ambush Thren's guild once they let down their guard near the very end of their raid. Remembering their screams still put a smile on Thren's face. With the building in ruins, it was easy work for Thren to crawl amid the ash on his belly, taking up vigil on Marion's home without anyone from the street possibly seeing him. He stared through a slit barely wider than his thumb, but he could see enough.

Knowing the rest of his guild waited on the rooftops, Thren cleaned ash off his apple, took a bite, and then settled in.

When the sun set, a very faint light shone in the window facing the street. It was a single candle, lit by Michael to let the rest know all was well inside. Thren smiled at the candle, and he let his nerves calm. Wallace and Michael were eyeing the streets as well. Should they spot a member of the Scorpions, then out the candle would go. Occasionally Thren watched someone wander down the street, more often than not a member of his guild. The stars twinkled into existence, and the city took on a bluish hue as the moon shone bright above it.

Yet as the hours passed, they saw not a sign of Carr's arrival.

I know you're patient, thought Thren as he shifted from side to side on his belly to keep his muscles loose. *But not this patient.*

Perhaps no one had run to Carr with information on Marion after all? Or perhaps Carr hadn't realized, when presented with the tip, that it'd actually been about Marion and not a decoy? Worse, what if they'd planned an ambush on Grayson after all? His friend was possibly the best living fighter he knew, but all the skill in the world meant nothing if an arrow took you through the back of the skull.

Thren shook his head, trying to banish the thoughts. Dozens of reasons could explain the delay, and dwelling on the worst of them did nothing. He had to focus on what he knew, and so far all he knew was that it was a quiet night in that little corner of Veldaren.

And then out went the candle.

"Where?" Thren breathed, pressing himself against the blackened wall. Across the rooftops he watched his guildmembers rise from their hiding spots, coming out through windows and up from false shingles. Several others rushed out from the alleyways, encircling the house. Yet despite it all, not a sign.

Dread clenched its cold fist around Thren's stomach, and he staggered to his feet, ignoring the aches from spending so many hours in one position. Stepping through the broken wall, he drew his swords as members of his guild neared.

"We saw no sign," said one, but Thren shook his head, hurrying toward the house.

"Inside," he said. "All of you, inside, now!"

When he reached the door, he heard Marion's scream. His foot slammed against the handle, and though it'd been locked, it broke under the force. The door opened a space, and using his shoulder for leverage, Thren smashed it open the rest of the way. He gave himself no time to think, no pause to survey the situation. It was time to act, and he whirled into motion. Two men were just before the door, small crossbows in hand. Their clothing was of the Scorpion Guild, and no doubt their arrows were tipped with the deadly poison of their namesake.

Thren flung himself to the left, lashing out with one of his short swords. One arrow sailed past him, embedding into the chest of one of his guildmembers behind him. The other bow failed to fire, Thren's sword smashing through its frail construction, snapping the string and cutting the arrow in half. Before either Scorpion could react, he flung himself back the other way, his swords dancing, opening up their throats with a shower of blood.

When they fell, Thren found himself face-to-face with Carr. The man looked harmless enough, his face round, his eyes a soft brown. But there was nothing soft about the dagger that pressed against his Marion's neck. Michael lay dead in the corner, an arrow lodged in his throat. By the window, his hand still resting atop the candle, was Wallace. The entire back of his shirt was soaked red.

"Not a step," Carr said. His voice was calm, as if they were good friends.

"Let her go," Thren said, the muscles in his body tensing.

"I said not a step." Carr pressed the dagger tighter against her throat, drawing a single crimson drop. From outside came screams, followed by the sound of combat. "Do you think you're the only one in Veldaren who knows how to plan an ambush?"

Thren looked to Marion, and she met his gaze. So far she had kept her mouth shut, but he could see by the fire in her eyes that she was just waiting for Carr to give her an opening. Even the slightest delay, and she would escape. Thren was not the only one who had grown up on the streets.

"How many men did you bring out there?" Thren asked, thinking to stall.

"Marion is mine," Carr said. "Which means ten or ten hundred, it doesn't matter, I have all the leverage I need right here."

"You lay a finger on her…"

"You'll what?" asked Carr. "Kill my wife? Cut a finger off little Reed's hand? They're not here, Thren, just you and me and Marion. Put down your swords, and fall to your knees."

"And if I don't?" asked Thren. He took a step closer, just to see how Carr reacted. The man didn't even flinch. "You'll kill Marion? Do it, and your family dies. Even if by a miracle you kill me as well, my orders will still stand. Grayson will execute both of them."

"Except Grayson's off stalking an empty warehouse," Carr said, and there was no hiding the victory in his voice. "And as for my family…you don't think I'd come after your wife without having freed my own, do you?"

The dread that had been building in Thren's stomach suddenly exploded throughout his body. That was it then. All his maneuvers, all his planning…it'd meant nothing. He'd thought he'd hidden Lenore and Reed somewhere Carr could never find them. He'd thought his ambush careful enough, and subtle enough, to suffice. But instead it'd all come crumbling down.

"You haven't won," Thren said.

"Yes," Carr said. "I have. Drop your swords."

"No." Thren took another step closer. "You're here, right here. No matter the territory, the gold, the reputation, or anything else, I know that you'd sacrifice all of it to save your life. And that's what's at stake right now, Carr. Harm her, and you die. It's that simple."

———

"And I know you," Carr said. "I know you'd never let something happen to Marion. No matter how fast you think you are, I'm the faster. On your knees, and drop your swords. I won't ask ag—"

"Carr!" shouted a Scorpion as he barged through the front door. "More Spiders coming in from the..."

Marion twisted in Carr's grasp, and Thren lunged. No one was faster than he was. He'd always believed it, worked hard training himself to be the absolute best. But it seemed time itself slowed so he might see the blur that was Carr's hand, see the spray of red that flew across the room, see the gap of flesh that was once his beautiful Marion's throat open up.

"No!" he screamed. He made to stab with his sword, but Carr flung Marion into his arms. Unable to help himself, he caught her, cradling her against him. She wasn't dead yet, the cut on her throat too shallow. As Carr fled into the second room of the house, Thren held her, stared into her dazzling blue eyes as the life slowly drained from them.

Thren shoved his cloak against her neck, trying to stem the bleeding. He heard her cough, try to speak. Her lips formed the words, and he read them easily enough.

Don't go.

Thren held her, looked to the other room. He felt his rage overwhelming him, felt his sorrow weighing down his shoulders. He didn't know what to do, what to say. Carr was getting away. That was all he could think about. The bastard was getting away.

Gently he put Marion down, cut off a shred of his cloak, and pressed it hard against her throat.

"I'll be back," he said, kissing her forehead.

When he ran into the other room, he found a latch open in the floor, the door lifted up to reveal a tunnel dug beneath the house. Thren heard Grayson's damning words echo in his head.

This was Scorpion territory for years…

A tunnel network. How many houses linked together? How many secret raids and transactions had been carried out through them, completely under Thren's nose? Not wanting to think on it, not wanting to let his mind realize how thoroughly he'd been outsmarted, Thren dropped into the tunnel. It was as dark a chasm as Thren had ever seen, but he was friends with the darkness. The tunnel went in only one direction, and on his hands and knees Thren crawled ahead. The sound of combat faded away, and on and on he rushed. His hands brushed the walls, following their gentle curves. In the growing silence, he listened for movements, for breathing, anything to signify Carr's presence.

After a curve, a yellow orb quickly came into view. It was a single stone, shining a puke yellow, but the light was enough for Thren to see that it shone directly above an intersection of two tunnels. Stopping beneath, Thren looked down all three passages, but they were nothing but empty walls of black. He tried to scan the ground, but there was no way to tell in what direction Carr had gone.

Curling his fingers into fists, he smashed them against the dirt and let out a bitter cry. Using the intersection for space, he turned around and crawled back to Marion. When he stood at the secret latch, he found several members of his guild standing around, waiting for him. Their weapons were bloodied, and many of the men were wounded. From the other room, Thren heard sobbing, and it took no guessing to know who it was.

"I'm sorry, Thren," said Senke, one of his more promising recruits. The handsome man reached down a hand, helping Thren climb out from the tunnel. "Grayson got us here too late."

Thren nodded. Feeling like a stranger in his own body, he stepped out into the other room. Grayson huddled over Marion's body, cradling her in his massive arms. Her eyes were closed. She did not move.

"Grayson..." Thren said. "I'm sorry. I should have known better. I should have..."

The man looked up.

"Damn it, Thren," he said, his voice hoarse. "You're not as good as you think you are. No one is, and now my Marion...now my little..."

Still holding his sister's body, he yanked the gray cloak off his shoulders and tossed it to the floor.

"I'm done with you," he said, rising to his feet, Marion's weight seemingly nothing as he held her. "You never listened, you bastard. Never thought someone could beat you. Maybe you'll learn again, maybe not, but I won't be here to find out. Take the whole damn city if you want. I'm gone."

He stormed out of the house, leaving Thren alone with the handful of his men.

Thren's fists shook as he closed his eyes and collected himself.

"What happened?" he asked.

"Warehouse was empty," Senke said. "Grayson didn't seem surprised at all. After that, we were going to return back to our hideout, but then we found this..."

Thren opened his eyes and accepted the offered item. It was a gray cloak, stained red and cut into several pieces.

"Grayson sent a runner to the safe house we had Carr's family locked up in, found it smashed open. The cloak belonged to one of the men stationed there. That's when Grayson sent us hurrying here. Managed to kill the rest of the Scorpions, at least those that didn't get away."

Thren crumpled the cloak in his hands. No doubt Carr had expected to get in and out of the home without being noticed, taking Marion with him. The cloak at the warehouse had been his way of taunting Thren, making sure he knew every single step of his plan had been expected or countered in some way.

"How many of you are there?" he asked Senke.

"Fifteen of us," the man said.

Thren drew one of his swords and scanned the faces of those with him. When he saw one in particular, he couldn't believe the audacity. Taking a step forward, he grabbed Pennell by the neck, yanked him to his knees, and then jammed a knee into the man's stomach.

"Carr tell you to stay and watch?" he asked as Pennell lay on the ground, clutching his waist. "He want you to tell him how miserable and beaten I was?"

"I don't know what you're..."

Thren kicked him in the teeth, silencing the lie. Reaching down, he grabbed Pennell's left hand, stretched it out, and then slammed his sword through the palm. It pierced the wood of the floor as Pennell screamed. The rest of the Spiders stepped away, some stunned by the revelation, others furious.

"Listen to me, you little shit," Thren whispered into the man's ear. "Someone will suffer my wrath tonight. It can be you, or it can be Carr. Now you fucking think long and hard about who you'd rather it be."

"The Raven's Claw," Pennell said, his face turning pale. "The upper levels, they're all Carr's. He'll be there, I swear!"

Thren stood, flipped his other short sword so he could grab the hilt with the blade downward, and jammed the blade down through Pennell's mouth. He let go of both his swords so he could stand and watch as Pennell convulsed. At last, when he was dead, Thren freed both weapons and cleaned off the blades.

"The Raven's Claw is a tavern in the far south," he told the men with him. His face felt flushed, yet his hands and feet like ice. "We're going there, now. I don't care who you see when we attack, whether or not you think them innocent. When we step inside their door, everyone dies. Everyone but Carr and his family. We take them alive. Do you understand?"

The hard eyes of hard men met his gaze, and they all nodded.

"Good," Thren said. "Then let's go."

They ran through the dark night streets, weapons drawn, cloaks fluttering behind them. The few who saw them coming fled quickly out of the way. No doubt many were in league with the Scorpions, but the Spiders ran too fast, too straight. No one would beat them. Thren wouldn't let them. Heart pounding, he let the blood coursing through his veins push away his thoughts of Marion, of the betrayal in Grayson's eyes. The chill of the night was a bitter kiss on his skin as the sweat ran down his neck.

They turned a corner, Thren still in the lead. The Raven's Claw tavern was in sight, a two-story construction lurking over the nearby homes. Lights shone through gaps in the curtains of the upper floors. Three burly men leaned against the front and side, looking bored. Guards, Thren knew, disguised as vagrants or drunkards. There was no disguising their panic when they saw the mass of gray cloaks come storming toward them.

"Never slow, never stop," Thren shouted as he drew his swords. "Faster than the night. Faster than the dead. Let the blood flow!"

The guards had fled inside by their arrival, but Thren wasn't worried. His mind had no space for worry. They'd come too fast, too hard. Carr couldn't outthink Thren at a game Thren was no longer playing. Arms crossed before his face, Thren slammed into the door, using his weight and momentum to smash it inward. As wood splintered around him he rolled, dodging frantic swings of swords by men on either side of the door. Pulling up from his roll, he lashed out, slicing out the throats of two men unlucky enough to be drinking at the table beside him. As they collapsed, Thren jammed his elbow onto the curved table, tipping it over as he fell once more. Arrows thudded into the table above him, fired by three men on the stairs with crossbows.

"Move!" Thren screamed at the door behind him. Glass shattered as his men smashed in through windows, others lunging through the doorway with their daggers drawn. The guards there were quickly overrun, and as the rest of the patrons drew their own weapons, Thren let out a laugh. What were they to him? Nothing, absolutely nothing.

The men on the stairs were busy reloading when several Spiders flung their daggers, killing one and wounding the two others. Thren saw this while glancing around the table, and with their threat over, he returned to his feet, short swords held out at either side of him. Behind the bar was another door, and pouring through it came members of the Scorpion Guild, all carrying long daggers or maces. Thren met their eyes as they leaped over the bar, trying to overwhelm the Spiders. This was the best they could do? The first to near him offered a clumsy thrust in an attempt to disembowel him, but Thren slapped it aside, stepped closer, and rammed his sword through the man's stomach.

"That's how you gut someone," Thren whispered into the man's ear, as if he were a dying lover. A twist, a yank, and the sword came free.

The rest of his guild clashed with the Scorpions, but these were Grayson's handpicked best, and they made short work of the frantic defenders. Blood spilled across the counter, and from every direction came screams. Thren reached behind the counter, grabbing several bottles, and then smashed them into a single puddle. That done, he grabbed a rag, soaked it with some of the liquid, and then dipped it into the fire as all around him men died. When the rag caught fire, he tossed it into the puddle, setting it aflame.

"Carr must be upstairs," Senke said, sliding up to him. His arms were caked with blood, as was his mace, and along his left cheek ran a weeping gash.

"Come with me," Thren said. "Send the rest outside to circle the place. No one escapes."

Senke shouted out the order as Thren climbed the stairs. At the top waited a trio of men, all wielding swords, their faces hidden behind the deep yellow of their cloaks and hoods. Behind them Thren caught a glimpse of an open door at the far end of the hall, and Carr running inside it.

"Do you smell the smoke?" Thren asked the men. "How well does a scorpion burn, I wonder?"

The first slashed with his sword, but it was a feint. The two others lunged as the man suddenly pulled back. Thren lifted his blades, and he could not keep the look of contempt off his face. He'd seen the other two tense, seen the way their feet shifted for their lunges, and the feint could not have been more obvious, for even if Thren had not blocked, the angle was such that the blow would have missed anyway.

If these were the best Carr had, Thren was sorely disappointed.

With his left hand he blocked one attack, and the other he parried aside so he could step closer, pull his sword around, and double-thrust for the man's stomach. Except instead of gaining an easy kill, he found his prey leaping away. The other two men converged simultaneously, one striking high, the other low. Thren let out a cry, and he fell back toward the stairs while batting aside the lower hit. Pain spiked across his chest, his shirt ripped and his chest bleeding from a shallow wound. Despite the pain, Thren let out a laugh. Perhaps Carr had at least one more trick left up his sleeve.

But now Thren knew the level of his foes. More importantly, he had help coming from the stairs. He rushed them headlong, swords a blur. They tried to cut him as he passed, but he shifted, angled his run so he flew through them, cloak hiding the bulk of his movements. Skilled they were, but Thren felt his mind sharpened, its focus magnified by the corpse of his beloved Marion. With every step, every hit, he felt his rage growing. Bleeding from more shallow cuts along his arms and legs, Thren landed on a shoulder, rolled to his back, and then kicked up to his feet.

"Not good enough," he said, spitting blood. From the stairs ran Senke, the way no longer blocked by Thren. Attackers on both sides, the three Scorpions tried to divide their attention, two to Thren, one to Senke. Neither had a chance. Senke was as skilled with his mace as any man could be with a weapon. He swung wide for the man's chest, but when he made to block, Senke had stepped in close, left leg sweeping out the man's knees. When the Scorpion fell, Senke's mace followed him to the ground, blasting in his ribs with an audible crunch.

———

Thren's two died just as easily, one sword finding throat, the other piercing lung. Yanking his blades free, Thren turned down the hall as smoke began to billow up the stairs.

"At my side," Thren said, ignoring the other doors as he ran. Finding the one on the far end, the one he'd seen Carr enter, he tested the handle and found it unlocked. Eyes narrowing, he turned the handle, kicked the door open, and then dodged to the side. An arrow shot through the center of the door, embedding into the opposite wall. Thren stepped inside, showing no hurry. Carr stood in a small but well-furnished bedroom. By the window stood Carr's wife, Lenore, and his ten-year-old son, Reed. Seeing Thren, the guildmaster lowered his empty crossbow.

"It wasn't supposed to happen this way," Carr said as Thren approached.

"I know," Thren said. "And I don't care."

*

They dragged all three through the street, their wrists bound together with rope. Of the fifteen Spiders who had come, only four had died, compared to the twenty Scorpions Thren's men had killed. No doubt more Scorpions lurked throughout the city, but Thren walked with his sword pressed against their leader's throat. None would dare interfere, not anymore. If anything, they'd all be looking for new guilds to take them in.

Thren said nothing to them, as did Carr. Lenore wept, the pretty little thing, but she kept her mouth shut. Only the child dared say anything, but his questions were ignored, and eventually he fell silent.

Arriving at Thren's hideout, a simple unmarked warehouse, they entered, Thren leading the way.

"Take them to the dark room," Thren ordered. "Tie them to the wall, but don't harm them needlessly."

As Thren watched the men carry out his orders, he glanced to the stairs leading to the upper floor. Waiting on them, watching quietly, were his sons. Aaron was barely visible over the bannister, his blond hair and blue eyes poking out. Beside him Randith leaned against the wall with his arms crossed, a frown on his face. He seemed so much more serious than his ten years should have allowed.

"Where's Mom?" Randith asked, his voice piercing the din.

Thren swallowed, tried to think of a way to answer.

"Dead," he said, his voice suddenly hoarse.

Randith winced, but he put on a show of remaining strong. It made Thren proud of him, sick as his stomach was from the finality of the words he'd spoken. Aaron, however, teared up immediately.

"No," the younger brother murmured. "No, she can't, she…"

"Take him back upstairs," Thren said. "Now. I have work to do."

Not wanting to see them any longer, to see their pain both hidden and obvious, he pushed his mind to the matters at hand. In the back of his warehouse was the dark room, unfurnished and lacking any windows. Thren stepped inside, taking a torch with him. Hooking it on the wall just below a small vent to allow the smoke to escape, he returned to the door and shut it. The sound it made echoed and echoed in the cramped space.

"Thren," Carr whispered, his features shadowed in the flickering torchlight. "Please, do whatever you want to me, but let them go. They had nothing to do with it, you know that. You know that!"

Tied to the opposite wall were Carr's wife and son, and they both sniffled, crying from fear and uncertainty. Thren never looked their way. Instead he stood before

Carr, let him see his body shaking with rage, let him see his control about to shatter.

And then Thren collapsed to his knees. He let his hardness break, let the anguish come pouring forth. As Carr watched in stunned silence, Thren beat against his legs, crying out Marion's name again and again. Stumbling to his feet, he flung himself against a wall and smashed his fists against it, then slammed it with his forehead. He thought of Marion's smile, her dazzling eyes. He remembered her body against his, every curve, every secret, all replaced by the ghost of a memory stolen away in Grayson's hands. Thren never bothered to wipe away his tears, just let them flow down his face, down his chin.

At last his composure came to him, almost unwillingly. Using his sleeve, he brushed the snot from his nose, then walked over to Carr. The man sat on his rear, with his hands tied above him, and Thren knelt so they might stare eye to eye.

"Listen well," Thren said after clearing his throat. "Tonight marks the end of your guild. Every Scorpion will die. Even those who left your guild to fly a cloak of a different color, they will die. Anyone who dares utter your name, or the name of your guild, will die. Twenty years from now, should a man be foolish enough to start a guild with the emblem of a Scorpion, I will crush his guild into the ground before it can last a week. Tonight you, and everything you accomplished, will cease to exist. Do you understand me, Carr?"

The man nodded, his jaw trembling.

Thren finally wiped at the tears that wetted his face, then held his hand out to Carr.

"I wanted you to see that," Thren said, his voice so soft, so cold. "I wanted you to see the pain and anguish you've caused me. Marion was everything to me. *Everything.*

My men may see me as hard, or calloused. Others will marvel at how I left her memory behind so easily. But you will know, Carr. You've seen it, seen every bit of my anguish."

Thren grabbed Carr by the hair and pulled him close enough that he could whisper into his ear.

"And you're about to feel that same pain and anguish, you stupid bastard. Because this isn't about the dead. This isn't about revenge. Not anymore. It's about the *message*."

He flung him back, rose to his feet. His tired, red-eyed gaze turned to Carr's terrified family. No smile, no pleasure on his face. A sob came from Carr's throat, yet the sound made no impact on Thren. Just a dullness in him now. A death.

"You'll feel it," Thren told the guildmaster. "I promise you, you'll feel it. All that pain. All that agony."

He drew his sword, approached the boy first.

"And I won't have to lay a hand on you to do it."

All throughout the night, Carr screamed and sobbed.

True to his word, Thren never laid a hand on him.

———

Cloak and Spider

Thren checked his things once more as he paced within a room of his safe house. His older son, Randith, was out with the rest of his guild, preparing for his own meeting that night. Much as it worried him, Thren knew Randith was seventeen now, and needed to handle certain things on his own. That meant waiting instead of organizing things himself. That meant pacing and drumming his fingers on the hilts of his swords as the minutes crawled on by, instead of rallying his Spider Guild for a potential war.

"You should be ashamed of yourself," Thren muttered, realizing just how nervous he was.

He went through a door leading to a modestly furnished bedroom, and was surprised to see his eight-year-old son, Aaron, standing there as if waiting for him. Thren raised an eyebrow, grunted.

"Yes?" he asked.

Aaron opened his mouth, closed it, and then looked to the ground. He was embarrassed about something, something he no doubt wanted to ask, but Thren didn't have the patience to wait it out. He noticed a book in his son's hand and he reached out and grabbed it. It was held open to a page with simple illustrations of a lioness and her cubs. It was a story Thren had seen his son reading multiple times, and he had a feeling as to why.

———

"I miss Mom," Aaron said when Thren looked up from the page. Thren shut the book and let out a sigh.

"We all do," he said, putting a hand on Aaron's shoulder. "But try not to let it overwhelm you."

He tossed the book to the bed and turned to leave, thinking their conversation over. Ever since Marion's death, Aaron had turned incredibly quiet and inward, rarely talking even with him. But it seemed that day was a day of surprises.

"Where are you going?" he asked before Thren could exit the door.

"I have things to do," he said.

"Randith?"

Thren turned back, nodded.

"Randith too. Why do you ask?"

Aaron rubbed an arm, bit his lower lip.

"What am I for?"

The question was so odd, so unexpected, it startled Thren. Taking in a deep breath, he let it out, forcing himself to relax, forced his impatience away and tried to be honest with his son for once.

"What do you mean?" he asked.

Aaron glanced away.

"You show Randith everything. You teach him every day. But not me. Why? What am I for?"

Thren crossed his arms, trying to decide on the right answer. Aaron was so young, but at times he seemed incredibly intelligent as well. Thren knew Randith might return anytime soon, but the mention of his beloved Marion had put a bit of nostalgia into his heart, and he sat down on the bed, gesturing for Aaron to sit beside him.

"I have some time to spare," he said, "so let me tell you a story. Perhaps that will help."

Aaron shifted in his seat and then hunched over, head rested on his hands, attentive. Thinking for a moment, Thren decided on the one he would tell.

"I was once told this story when I was younger," he said. "When I was still being trained by the Darkhand. My version will be a little different, but still similar. It's the story of the cloak and the spider.

"Years ago, when this land was still in its infancy, there was a man who'd been gifted with a cloak from a powerful wizard. The cloak made him wise, and made his life last for centuries. But this man had walked the land since its creation, and he was tired. Tired of the strife. Tired of watching his loved ones pass away while he continued on. So he rented a room from a farmer, and then in the middle of the night he stole away to the barn. There he built a fire, removed his cloak, and tossed it into the flames. The cloak burned to ash, and the man smiled, aged to dust, and then died.

"The cloak, however, did not burn completely. A tiny bit of it burned loose and floated on the wind, circling around the barn until it caught in the web of a small spider. That spider didn't know what had happened, but he was suddenly aware now, far more wise than a simple spider should be. He looked at his little web and decided it could be bigger. It could be stronger. So the spider cast his web out farther, no longer taking up just a tiny little corner but instead larger and larger pieces of the roof.

"The farmer saw him building, and at first it just amused him. Spiders kept away the bugs, ate the flies, things he was never fond of anyway. But the spider continued to build, eating the little flies and moths and things that fly about. And he lived, lived far longer than a spider should have. He grew wiser, and he wrapped that piece of cloak into the very center of his web, knowing that it must be carefully protected, and that the spider must never leave his web. He also learned to strike fast, for the insects caught in his web would gain the same wisdom.

"So larger and larger the spider grew. He took a mate, one he loved dearly, and he made her a promise. So long as she remained safe in the heart of his web, he would spin her a creation so majestic she would understand how greatly he loved her. And so he did, crawling, spinning, until the farmer saw it and was afraid. But the spider was bigger now, the size of a fist, and the farmer was a cowardly man. He struck at his web at times, hacked parts of it with sticks should it get in his way, but he tried to ignore the spider, figuring surely the spider would soon die."

"The farmer wasn't wise, was he?" Aaron asked. Thren chuckled, but before he could answer he realized Aaron had leaned against him, the weight of his body pressing against his chest. It seemed strange, and he realized just how little contact he had with his own son. Clearing his throat, Thren began again, hiding his discomfort.

"No, he wasn't," Thren continued. "If he had been wise, he would have crushed the spider the moment he realized something was amiss. But he didn't, and the spider grew and grew. He fed on bats and small birds, and everything made him larger. Soon the barn itself was wrapped entirely in his webs, and the farmer would not go there anymore. Larger birds, owls and hawks, began to get trapped within the web. But the spider was still not happy. He was hungry, so hungry. He cast his web to the ground, catching dogs, wolves, groundhogs, trapping them, wrapping them, feeding upon them. His legs grew larger, and each eye like the pit of a peach. Yet his mate remained small as she always was, resting peacefully in the heart of the web.

"But then…then something terrible happened. The spider felt a shaking of his web, and normally that meant yet another captured prey, but this time it was deep in its center. He tried to hurry back, but he was so large, so lumbering now. By the time he arrived, there was only terror in every one of his eight eyes: his beloved mate was dead, stung by a scorpion that had crawled up from the ground."

Aaron shivered. Thren started to speak, found a lump in his throat. He closed his eyes, breathed out slowly.

"The spider had erred," he said. "He'd cast his web throughout the barn, but missed a piece of dirt directly below the heart of it. And he was heartbroken, and lost, and confused. He vowed to never again make such a mistake. Outward he cast his web, bathing the ground in white. From the barn he went, for there would be web everywhere now, stretching across the hills to the very sun itself. When the spider crawled out from the barn for the first time in years, the farmer fled, terrified by the very sight of it. Wolves, serpents, cattle in the fields, deer in the forests, eagles in the sky: they were all trapped and devoured. Nothing stopped his hunger. The webs were like great ropes, and the slightest touch would forever trap you.

"At last the farmer returned, and he did not come alone. Other farmers, men who had lost cattle and hens, accompanied him bearing torches. Soldiers from the king came as well, with swords and shields, for they had been told all the terrible stories of the spider that had claimed all the land as its own. They took their torches to the web, slowly burning toward the web's center. The spider sensed them coming, and he did not run. He was too tired now, his legs like thin trunks of trees. He rushed them, still fast for something of such size, and fought with all his strength. As the torches burned his body he buried his teeth into body after body, flooding them with venom. The spikes at the bottoms of his legs slashed open bodies, and he thrashed and thrashed, spinning web for miles all around, burying hundreds, their only salvation that of a torch's fire to burn them to death before starvation."

Thren looked to his hands, opened and closed them.

"And then the spider died," he said. "Too big, too old, too tired."

Aaron shifted, and he no longer leaned against his father. His face was passive, but Thren could see the faintest hint of a frown on his son's face.

"That's a horrible story," he said.

Thren chuckled.

"The story is not finished," he said, standing.

"Then how does it end?"

Thren knelt before his son, and strangely he felt tears coming to his eyes. He took his son's hands in his, squeezed them tight.

"For though the spider died, his children clung to his back. They crawled from his body and onto the web, and they too gained the wisdom from the cloak. And as they looked about, they found a nation covered with webs. They found bountiful food waiting for them, and a thousand places they might hide should any come looking for them. Everything they could want, prepared so carefully by the spider. All but one. A small little spider remained on the body, frightened to move to the web. Frightened of the wisdom of the cloak. It stayed there with the body of its father, content, until one day that smallest spider finally climbed down to the web, the bravest of them all, the wisest. That is how the story ends."

———

He stood, moved to the door. From the other side he heard movement, and when he opened it he found Randith coming in from the street.

"Everything's prepared for my meeting with Maynard Gemcroft," Randith said, adjusting his sword belt. "Are you ready for yours?"

"I am," Thren said. "I'm sure Leon will be unpleasant as it is, but if we want to prevent this coming war, we should go swiftly, before he thinks we purposefully left him waiting."

"Then let's head out."

Randith returned to the exit, and Thren made to follow. Aaron stopped him before he could.

"Wait," he said. "What becomes of the children?"

Thren turned, smiled at him.

"All legends must have their heir," he said. "The children who rushed off on their own became equals of their father, as he had always hoped. But the one who waited, the one who learned, the one who finally had the courage to brave the cloak...that small little spider grew a legend all his own."

Note from the Author:

This is a small collection, so I promise a small note. People have sent me requests for Thren's backstory, and while I've dabbled into bits of it (such as with Grayson in *A Dance of Shadows*), there's a lot of little stories I've never found the chance to tell. I've been accused of making Thren one-dimensional, just a mindless hateful killing machine, and this is one of many attempts to help flesh him out beyond being just the monster that raised the Watcher.

Also, those of you who have long been asking me who trained Thren, now you have your answer, at least a sliver of it with the reveal of Muzien the Darkhand. I have far more planned for this character, so consider this a taste prior to the release of *A Dance of Ghosts*.

Hope you all enjoyed, despite the grimness near the end. Depending on how well received these stories are, I might consider doing another collection for a different character (Tarlak Eschaton, maybe, or Deathmask...). Until then, thanks for giving me yet another chance to dabble in the world of these characters I love.

David Dalglish
May 30, 2013

CPSIA information can be obtained
at www.ICGtesting.com
Printed in the USA
LVHW03s0053030818
585752LV00004B/741/P

9 781500 374822